"Just let your feelings take over," Jake said

"We may not like each other, Lisle, but I'm ready to bet any money that we have a common meeting ground just the same."

He touched her face, his thumb caressing the soft curve of her cheek, his fingers discovering the delicacy of her jawline.

He said quietly, "If it's any consolation, I never intended this to happen, either."

He took her into his arms quite gently, not kissing her, just holding her against the hard lean length of his body. She knew by the pressure of Jake's body against hers that he was deeply and hotly aroused. It was exciting to know that she was wanted, and she evinced no kind of protest as his hands slid down her body to her slender hips, molding her against him, because she knew that she wanted to be even closer still.

Books by Sara Craven

HARLEQUIN PRESENTS

HARLEQUIN ROMANCES

These books may be available at your local bookseller.

For a free catalog listing all titles currently available,
send your name and address to:

Harlequin Reader Service
2504 West Southern Avenue, Tempe, AZ 85282
Canadian address: Stratford, Ontario N5A 6W2

SARA CRAVEN

a bad enemy

Harlequin Books

TORONTO • NEW YORK • LONDON
AMSTERDAM • PARIS • SYDNEY • HAMBURG
STOCKHOLM • ATHENS • TOKYO • MILAN

Harlequin Presents first edition December 1983
ISBN 0-373-10647-5

Original hardcover edition published in 1983
by Mills & Boon Limited

CHAPTER ONE

'WONDERFUL party, darling,' the man said. He was smiling owlishly and slurring his words, and Lisle wondered without interest who he was. A friend of Janie's, perhaps. Certainly no one she knew.

'Thank you.' She gave him an absent smile and tried to move past him down the passage to the kitchen. 'It's not a wonderful party,' she thought. 'It's a lousy party, and I'm bored out of my skull. I wish they'd all go.'

She was amazed to hear herself. She was the girl who enjoyed life to the full, who only needed a few hours' sleep, whose pace never slackened.

'I'm starting to believe my own publicity,' she thought ruefully.

'Where are you goin'?' The man seized her arm, his face plaintive. His fingers felt warm and clammy on her skin, and she had to repress a shiver of distaste.

She tried to detach herself, but he hung on. 'To get some more ice.' She kept her voice cool and equable, because she didn't know who he was. Someone had once made a semi-drunken pass at her at a party, and she'd administered a crushing snub and a slapped face, only to discover when taxed on the matter by a furious Gerard that he had been an important client, and she had just lost Harlow Bannerman a contract that they had wanted. Since then, she had learned to handle the casual fondling, the innuendoes and sometimes blatant propositioning with imperturbable charm. As Gerard had pointed out, it was part of her job.

'Don' leave me,' the man said, and winked at her. 'I've been trying to get you alone all evening.'

She doubted that. The truth was probably that he

had seen her slip out of the room and followed, fancying his chances, and now he was blocking the way to the kitchen and leering.

She groaned inwardly, and at the same moment the doorbell pealed loudly. Saved by the bell, she told herself drily, inwardly blessing the late arrival.

She threw the front door open, smiling with determined gaiety, but the man on the threshold didn't smile back. In fact the expression on his face was almost one of contempt, which was ridiculous considering he was a complete stranger to her.

Lisle wondered for a moment if he was a new neighbour coming to complain about possible noise, because he wasn't a party guest, or even a hopeful gatecrasher. Instinct told her that.

He said, 'Miss Bannerman?'

She went on smiling. 'Yes?'

A dark forbidding face, she thought, the features harshly marked, with a firm-lipped mouth and a nose which had quite evidently been broken at some time in its career, but attractive nonetheless.

He said, 'Perhaps we could have a private word—preferably out of earshot of that—bear-garden.' He waved towards the muted roar of the party.

'Oh dear.' Lisle raised her eyebrows. 'So who are you? The police—the bailiffs—the Inland Revenue?—because whoever you are, I think you've got the wrong person.'

He shook his head, the wintry grey eyes going impassively over her, taking in every detail of the expensive black dress from the low neckline to the skirt slit as far as her thigh.

'I don't think so.' There was a sudden burst of noisy laughter from the living room, and he glanced towards the half-closed door, his mouth twisting. 'And how will this ultimately feature in the Harlow Bannerman accounts?' he asked. 'As entertaining clients?'

'My God!' Lisle struck a pose of exaggerated

horror. 'It *is* the Inland Revenue!' The owlish man released his grip on her arm and slid back to the party, leaving them alone in the narrow hall, watching each other warily.

She said, 'All joking apart, would you mind telling me who you are, and what you want?'

'In privacy—yes.' He walked past her unhurriedly, down the passage, away from the din of the party. 'In here, perhaps.' He opened a door.

'And perhaps not,' Lisle said indignantly. 'That happens to be my bedroom.'

He said grimly, 'Spare me the coy protests, Miss Bannerman, they don't go with your clothes. I assure you I'm not in the mood, and even if I were, you overestimate your charms where I'm concerned.'

The breath caught in her throat. She said slowly, 'I—think I've just been—insulted. Will you leave now, or must I have you thrown out?'

'You have to have me thrown,' he said at once. 'And before you do perhaps I should tell you that your grandfather was taken ill this afternoon, and is asking for you. He isn't expected to live.'

She made a muffled sound and sank down on the bed, pressing her hand against her mouth, her green eyes widening in shocked incredulity.

She exclaimed, 'This afternoon? But why has no one been in touch—why wasn't I told before?'

'You could have been,' he said, 'if you entertained less, or left your phone on the hook more. I've been trying to make contact for several hours. In the end I decided it would be easier to come in person and fetch you myself.'

'Breaking the news to me gently *en route*,' she said in a shaky breath.

'You're tough, Miss Bannerman. You can take it.' But the grim note in his voice told her it would make little difference to him whether she could or not.

'Who are you?' she demanded.

'Jake Allard,' he said. 'You may or may not have heard of me.'

She'd heard of him all right, but she'd never bargained for meeting him, and the shock of it drove the breath out of her body for a moment. Gerard had confidently insisted that he was no longer a threat, but here, in the confined space of her bedroom, he seemed about as threatening as it was possible to get.

'You seem lost for words,' he observed, after a pause. 'How about "I thought you were in the States"?'

Her lips parted to deny all knowledge of him, or interest in him or his movements, and then closed again.

'Very wise.' He sounded faintly amused for the first time. 'I wouldn't have believed you. I'm sure that brother of yours has been keeping you well up to date on the whole situation.'

Not, she thought, if you're here when he thinks you're in America.

It was over a year since Gerard had first mentioned Jake Allard's name. At that time, he had been no more than a cloud no bigger than a man's hand on the Harlow Bannerman horizon, but in the months which followed, he had assumed ever larger and more ominous proportions.

'He wants the company,' Gerard had stated flatly. 'Allard International have a small electronics subsidiary of their own, and he wants to expand it. We have the know-how that he needs, but he doesn't want to pay for it. He knows that we've been badly hit by the recession and he reckons if he waits long enough he can pick us up for peanuts. That's of course if Grandfather doesn't invite him to join the Board anyway.'

Lisle had given him a swift anxious glance. 'You think that's likely?'

'I wish I didn't.' Gerard lit a cigarette and puffed at it edgily. 'But when I got back from Rome last week, Oliver Grayson told me they were practically living in each other's pockets.' He added furiously, 'He seemed delighted.'

Oliver Grayson would, of course. He had all the respect in the world for their grandfather Murray Bannerman, who had built the company up from nothing, and he had been close to their father too, but he had never made any secret of the fact that he felt it was time the family control over the firm ran out, and that Gerard would achieve his ambition of becoming managing director, and ultimately, the chairman only over his dead body. A solution which would suit Gerard perfectly well, Lisle thought drily.

Oliver Grayson wouldn't altogether object if Harlow Bannerman became part of the expanding Allard empire. He must have been desperately disappointed when all the talk in the financial papers of takeovers and mergers quietly died away, and Gerard announced that Jake Allard had gone to the States to open a new research laboratory, adding with satisfaction that there had been a slight rise in the value of Harlow Bannerman shares.

Now Lisle looked at Jake Allard, her face expressionless.

'I take it that you've been at the Priory.'

'A private visit, at your grandfather's invitation.' He gave her a faint smile. 'So, if you're trying to pin the blame for this latest attack on to me, forget it. You know as well as I do what a sick man he's been, and I'd say that your brother's machinations, and your increasingly public performances haven't done a great deal to contribute to his well-being.' He eyed her levelly for a moment. 'So now perhaps you could get a move on, unless being stubborn and obstructive is a trait you share with your brother.'

Lisle opened one of the fitted cupboards which ran the length of one wall, dragged out a weekend case, and began to hurl things into it, almost at random. She was trying to keep her temper under control, to concentrate on the thought of her grandfather and her concern for him.

Because he had always been the rock in her life. Her mother had died when she was born, and as her father had been a charming lightweight who had preferred travelling the world, selling Harlow Bannerman, rather than providing a stable home background for two growing children, Lisle and Gerard had been brought up instead at the Priory, under Murray Bannerman's aegis.

But now the rock was crumbling, and she felt the stirrings of a blind panic within her. She retrieved a scent spray from the dressing table and in the mirror she saw Jake Allard reflected, watching her, the grey eyes icily inimical, and the panic grew.

She said, 'Does Gerard know?'

'He seems to have disappeared,' he drawled. 'I've set Grayson on to look for him, but perhaps you can help us trace him. I imagine he's on one of his expense account forays after someone else's wife.'

She raised her eyebrows scornfully. 'A puritan, Mr Allard? How unusual!'

'In your circle, without a doubt.' His hard mouth twisted. 'But I'm no puritan, sweetheart, so don't push your luck. I'm quite prepared to believe that you share your brother's alleycat standards.'

Lisle was holding her hairbrush. It was a heavy one, silver-backed, and she threw it at him with all her strength. He dodged without haste, and fielded it neatly to her chagrin.

'Red hair and a temper to match,' he said softly. 'Well, control it when I'm around, Miss Bannerman, or I shall take this brush and apply it hard to a portion of your spoiled anatomy. Do I make myself clear?'

'More than clear.' Her rounded breasts were rising and falling stormily, but most of her anger was directed at herself. She should have stayed cool, not allowed him to get at her, or at least let him know that he had done so. She swallowed, steadying her breathing deliberately. 'I'm going to change now, so perhaps you'd leave the room.'

He lifted one shoulder in a negligent shrug. 'If you feel it's necessary.' His gaze slid mercilessly down her body. 'That dress, after all, leaves little to the imagination.'

'But fortunately,' she snapped, 'not everyone has your brand of imagination!'

The door was flung open, and Janie appeared on a little breeze of resentment. 'I thought you were supposed to be getting more ice. Alan's drink is practically coming to the boil. . . .' She stopped dead. 'Oh dear,' she went on after a well-judged pause. 'I appear to be interrupting something. Lisle darling, you really should learn to lock your door.'

'You're interrupting nothing,' Lisle said wearily, noticing Janie's eyes bright with malicious interest. She was used to Janie. Jake Allard wasn't, and she knew that crack about the locked door would have been noted and filed away for future reference. 'I'm sorry about the ice. As it happens, I've got to break up the party. I'm going away for a few days.'

'Now that is fast work!' Janie's incredibly long mascaraed lashes were fluttering as if they'd been caught in a gale. 'Not that I blame you, darling, not for one moment.' She sent Jake Allard one of her deliberately provocative sexy looks, and he laughed suddenly, the harsh lines of his face softening into genuine amusement.

When he wasn't being a bastard, he could be diabolically attractive, Lisle realised wonderingly.

She said quietly, 'Janie, Grandfather's dying.'

For a second her flatmate's face wore an expression of almost ludicrous astonishment. 'But he can't be, darling! He's Murray Bannerman. He's immortal—everyone knows that.' In one of her mercurial changes of mood, she was sober suddenly, taking control. 'You look ghastly. I'll finish your case.' She looked at Jake Allard. 'Perhaps you'd get Lisle a drink. She looks as if she could do with a brandy. And yourself, of course.'

'Not now, thanks. I've a long drive ahead.' He went out, closing the door behind him.

Janie swept up a handful of underwear and tucked it into the corner of the case. 'Who was that?'

'Jake Allard.' Lisle was feeling limp again. She sat down on the dressing stool.

'My word! No wonder his face seemed familiar.'

'You know him?'

'Graham does.' That was her boss. 'And I've seen the odd blurred pic in the financial pages. According to all reports, he's dynamite, and not only in the boardroom.'

Lisle grimaced slightly. 'That doesn't altogether surprise me.'

Janie folded Lisle's nightdress with exaggerated care. 'Does the fact that he's here mean that the deal is on again with Harlow Bannerman?'

'I don't know.' Lisle shook her head slowly. 'I dare not think. Everything's happening too fast—and Gerard's vanished.'

'You don't know where he is?' Janie's eyes were on her face.

Lisle shrugged. 'I could make an educated guess.' Barbados, she thought. That was where Gerard would be, with Carla Foxton. Mrs Carla Foxton. A wave of irrational anger at Jake Allard swept over her. Oh, damn him, he had a reputation of his own, so what right had he to sit in judgment on anyone else?

'Then I'd get him back if I were you. This is not a good time for him to be missing, believe me.' Janie was unwontedly sober, and Lisle bit her lip.

'Is it that bad?' She tried for lightness of tone, and didn't quite make it.

'It could be.' Janie gave a little shake of her head. 'I'm sure Gerard would rather be here, fighting, than coming back to salvage what he can from the wreckage.

For that's all there'd be, and you can ask Graham if you don't believe me.'

'Oh, I believe you,' Lisle said bitterly. 'I believe you only too well. The Allard man looks capable of anything.'

'And in this case appearances aren't deceptive,' Janie said grimly. 'According to all reports, he's fought his way single-handed up a very steep ladder, and you don't do that these days without stepping on a number of faces.'

'By the look of him, he's also been trodden on in his time,' Lisle said caustically. 'I'd like to shake the hand of the man who did it.'

'I don't recommend it.' Janie shot her a minatory glance. 'My advice is to forget that you don't find him the flavour of the month—particularly if he's going to be a force to be reckoned with in Harlow Bannerman. Graham says that Jake Allard can be a good friend—but a very bad enemy.'

'Indeed?' Lisle had discarded the black dress by now, and was pulling a cashmere sweater over her head to match the olive green corded jeans. She tugged the sweater into place, and raked her fingers carelessly through the heavy waves of copper hair, pushing it back into shape. 'Well, perhaps he'll discover the same can be said of me.' She cast a swift glance over the contents of the case and remembered her toilet bag from the bathroom. 'He doesn't frighten me,' she flung over her shoulder as she went to the door.

Jake Allard was coming down the passage, glass in hand. There was no way he couldn't have heard her last remark, and his teeth glinted momentarily in a faint, hard smile as he held the glass out to her.

'Your brandy, Miss Bannerman, or perhaps the need for it has passed.'

She said curtly, 'Yes, it has,' and went on down the passage to the bathroom.

It was unoccupied, and obeying an impulse she

hardly understood, she closed the door behind her, and shot the small bolt, shutting herself in away from the rest of the world. There was a mixture of exotic scents in the warm air, and several of the towels lay damp and crumpled on the floor. Automatically she retrieved them, straightening them and returning them to the heated handrail. There were mirrors everywhere and she seemed to catch sight of herself in them all, a myriad reflections of Lisle, two bright spots of colour in her pale face, her green eyes glittering like a cat's.

She'd spoken brave words, but they had been a lie. Of course she was frightened, with a deep gut-wrenching panic which was totally outside her experience. She felt as if every prop and stay to her security were being knocked away one by one, and there was nothing she could do to prevent it.

She sank down on the high-backed wicker chair and tried to think, to reason out everything which had happened in the past hour.

Grandfather, she had been told, could be dying, but then his doctors had written him off before, and been wrong. As Janie had said, Murray Bannerman was immortal. He didn't believe in illness, or particularly in safeguarding his health against the march of time either.

'If you lived as these damned medicos want you to, you might as well be dead,' he had growled testily more than once.

The doctors grumbled too about his refusal to follow their advice, his frankly avowed aversion to hospitals, They complained it was impossible to give him the treatment he needed, but Lisle knew that secretly they admired his stubbornness and his fighting spirit.

She tried to imagine life without him—Harlow Bannerman without him, and the exhilarating board-room battles he had always enjoyed. She had often felt he secretly relished the covert sniping between Gerard and Oliver Grayson, but she had never until then doubted for a moment whose side he would be on if ever the chips were down.

Now she was not so sure.

Jake Allard at the Priory—on a private visit. And just what discussions had gone on under the shelter of that privacy? she wondered desperately. It was surely beyond coincidence that all this should have taken place when Gerard was safely out of the way, so what could her grandfather have been thinking of?

She would have to telephone Gerard somehow, get him back into the country before it was too late.

He'd covered his tracks well if Jake Allard had failed to find him, she thought, but it was hardly surprising. Harry Foxton wasn't over-jealous, or particularly suspicious, but he was no fool either, and any hint that Gerard and Carla were enjoying a break from a damp English autumn on the same Caribbean island would set all kinds of alarm bells ringing. Few men with very attractive wives trusted Gerard, she was forced to admit.

But it wasn't altogether his fault, she thought loyally. Since childhood, he had always been too good-looking and possessed of far too much charm for his own good. His hair was darker than hers—a kind of rich chestnut, and his eyes were bluer, and he had the look of a young Renaissance prince. Women had begun drooling over him in his pram, and almost before he had left adolescence the admiring looks had become frankly speculative. It was like letting a child loose in a sweetshop, Lisle thought ruefully. And so far he had shown no sign of surfeit. . . .

She sighed. She knew the fact that Gerard had laughed to scorn any idea that he should settle down and give some thought to the next generation of Bannermans had distressed her grandfather. Murray Bannerman believed in the family, and the stability of marriage. He had said openly that a wife and child might give Gerard the sense of responsibility he so often seemed to lack, and yet at the same time he usually greeted the rumour of some new romantic adventure by his grandson with a muttered, 'The young dog!' and a hoarse chuckle.

Lisle's attitude to Gerard's constant affairs fell a long way short of approval, but he was her older brother, and although there was now no trace of the hero-worship with which she had regarded him when they were much younger, she loved him and made mental excuses for his faults, even when his selfishness and lack of consideration impinged upon herself.

And if there was to be a battle between him and Jake Allard for the control of Harlow Bannerman, she would be fighting at Gerard's side all the way, she told herself angrily.

Someone rattled the bathroom door and retreated with a muffled curse, and Lisle started to her feet, seizing her brown quilted bag and filling it rapidly with essential toilet items. She wondered how long she would be staying at the Priory. Until. . . . Her mind closed down, refusing to admit the rest of the thought.

Her only comfort as she unbolted the door and went slowly back to the bedroom was that Murray was a fighter too.

Janie was alone when she went in, and she looked at her, a mute question in her eyes.

'He's gone to get his car.' She zipped the case shut and held it out to Lisle. 'You'll need a jacket or something.'

'Yes.' She had a new one, dark brown supple suede with a deep fur trim on the collar and cuffs, and now seemed as good a time as any to wear it. She needed the reassurance that something new, expensive and glamorous could give her.

She swung her bag over her shoulder, draped the coat over her arm and picked up her case. Janie followed her out of the room and along to the front door. Lisle gave her a taut smile.

'Perhaps you should get back to our guests,' she said, 'before they drink us dry and start wrecking the place.'

Janie nodded, biting her lip. She said gently, 'Take it easy, love. Remember what I said.'

'I'm not likely to forget it,' Lisle said ruefully.

As she pushed open the glass door and emerged on to the street, the car pulled up at the kerbside, and Jake Allard got out. He opened the passenger door, and stood impassively, waiting for her to cross the pavement to his side, the slight chill of the breeze ruffling the thick blackness of his hair.

Lisle had to force herself to move. She felt drained of strength so that walking became almost an effort of will alone. The only thing which kept her from falling down was the sure and certain knowledge of who would pick her up again, because, crazily, the prospect of being touched by him was suddenly the worst threat of all.

When he reached for her case, to stow it in the trunk, she pretended she hadn't seen the gesture, and put it down on the pavement in front of him instead. She was so uptight that even an accidental brush of fingers could well make her fall apart.

The car was capacious, the front seats well spaced, but when he closed her door and came round to take his place behind the wheel, she felt claustrophobic. She lifted a hand and eased the high collar of her sweater away from her tight throat, making herself breathe deeply.

Jake Allard gave her a frowning glance. 'You should have had that brandy,' he said curtly. 'There's a flask in the glove compartment.'

'I'm fine,' she said off the top of her voice, then added, 'Thank you.'

'You look like hell,' he informed her brutally. 'What good is it going to do Murray to see you like this? Or is he used to it?'

Lisle set her teeth. 'If we could just go?'

She'd hoped, childishly, that he would turn out to be a lousy driver, flashy, aggressive and impatient with other motorists, but of course, he was none of those things. Of course. She sat, hating him, across London, glad to be able to build on her anger because it kept the anxiety at bay.

He didn't say much. Once he asked her if she had any preference as to the route they took, and later, if she wanted some music.

She said, 'The quickest, preferably,' to the first question, and, 'Yes, please,' to the second. Otherwise there was silence, only faintly disguised by the music.

In other circumstances, in other company she would have enjoyed the tapes. They were obviously of his own devising, and expertly done, and she couldn't fault the choices he'd made either, although she wasn't familiar with them all. Jack Jones, she recognised, and Carly Simon and Judy Tzuke. With any other man, that could have been a talking point, the first tentative stage in an acquaintance that might or might not develop into a relationship. But not with this man.

Every word he had said to her, every look he had given her was etched on her mind, and the acid had bitten deep.

Darkness had closed around them, and the street lights dwindled as the roads narrowed into lanes.

Lisle sat up suddenly, peering around her. 'This isn't the way to the Priory.'

'He isn't at the Priory,' he said shortly. 'He's in intensive care in hospital.'

Lisle's hand stole to her lips, stifling a sharp sound of distress. She said, 'He hates—machines.'

'So I gathered.' His tone was dry. 'But this time it wasn't up to him to decide. And considering it was a matter of life and death, it was probably just as well.'

She said sharply, 'If Murray is going to die, which I don't necessarily accept, then he'd rather it was with dignity in his own bed than strapped up to some—electronic miracle.'

'And if the electronic miracle were to live up to its name and save him—how would you feel then?'

She sank back in her seat, biting her lip. In a low voice she said, 'He's an old man, and this isn't the first attack he's had. I don't think I—believe in miracles.'

'I'd be interested to know what beliefs you do hold, if any,' said Jake Allard. 'But that can wait. In the meantime, perhaps you could control your most obvious doubts, especially in front of Murray.'

'Of course I will!' she said indignantly. 'What do you take me for?' As soon as the words were spoken, she could have kicked herself.

She didn't have to look at him to know he was smiling.

'Another point for discussion at a later date, Miss Bannerman.'

Her hands clenched in her lap, the nails curling involuntarily into her palms. Was it possible that Murray could trust this man, like him—even tolerate him?

She saw the lights of the hospital in the distance with a strong feeling of relief. She would soon be rid of him, she thought. No doubt he had come to fetch her to Murray's bedside out of consideration for the older man, but as Murray's collapse had necessarily curtailed the discussions they had been having, there was no reason for him to linger, as she was prepared to make more than clear.

As the car turned in between the tall gates, she said, 'I'd be grateful if you could drop me at the main entrance.'

'I hate to pass up a novelty like your gratitude,' he said. 'But I'm afraid I can't do as you request. I'm putting the car in the car park, and then we're going in to see Murray together.'

Her voice shook with temper. 'Forgive me, but aren't

you taking this togetherness thing a little too far? I'm sure you—intend to be kind,' she added with heavy irony, 'but from here on in, I'm sure Murray would prefer to see only members of his immediate family.'

'Namely you and your brother, whenever he turns up.' Jake Allard swung the car deftly into a spot between two other vehicles, and braked.

'As a matter of fact, yes.'

He shook his head, as he switched off the lights and the ignition, and pocketed the keys. 'I'm afraid it isn't as simple as that, Miss Bannerman. There are other factors to be taken into account.'

'Such as your overweening desire for control of Harlow Bannerman,' Lisle asked sarcastically. 'You can hardly badger Murray with business propositions now.'

'I never did,' he said flatly. 'All the initial approaches have been made by him. Whatever your brother may choose to think, it's Harlow Bannerman that needs Allard International at this juncture, and not the other way round. You're a member of the company, Miss Bannerman, and a shareholder, presumably. Don't you ever look at reports and balance sheets? I recommend that you do so, and in the near future. It could be instructive.'

She fumbled for the door catch, and the door swung open.

'I don't want to hear any more of this,' she said, as she got out. 'I'm going to see my grandfather. He's all I need to know about right now.'

She had long legs and she strode out, hoping that he would take the hint and stay where he was, but when she reached the electronically operated sliding doors to the main foyer, he was beside her.

Lisle turned to him, her face frozen. 'This is getting ridiculous.'

'I quite agree,' he said grimly. 'Perhaps before you go rushing off in all directions to intensive care, you might care to listen to me for a moment. There's something you ought to know.'

She looked up into the harshly unsmiling face, her green eyes widening. 'There are—other complications? He can't—oh no, he can't be—dead already, and you haven't told me?'

'Of course not. But you're right that there are complications—although it's true to say that Murray is causing them, not suffering from them.'

Lisle felt unutterably weary. She slid a hand round the nape of her neck, freeing her heavy fall of copper hair from the confines of her coat collar.

'All the complications seem to be in your head, Mr Allard. Could you explain more clearly, if you must, and a damned sight more quickly.'

'Last time I gave you bad news, Miss Bannerman, you complained because I didn't break it to you gently.'

'Oh, I'm not listening to any more of this!' Lisle turned away impatiently, but he detained her, taking her arm, not gently, and pulling her round to face him.

'Yes, you are,' he grated. 'You're going to listen, you spoiled little brat, so that if Murray is conscious and able to speak, you'll be able to tell him what he wants to hear.'

'That I'm delighted he's apparently selling out to you?' Lisle demanded, green eyes sparkling. 'The words would choke me.'

'Then chew them well,' he came back at her, his mouth twisting. 'Because it's no business deal he wants you to approve. What Murray's waiting to hear is that I've asked you to marry me—and that you've agreed.'

CHAPTER TWO

THERE was a long screaming silence.

At last, Lisle said huskily, 'You—cannot be serious.'

Jake Allard said with a kind of weary impatience, 'Is it likely I'd be joking—about such a thing—and at a time like this?'

She looked at him blankly. 'But Murray couldn't—he wouldn't. . . .'

'Wrong on both counts, I'm afraid.' The grey eyes flickered over her, then still holding her arm Jake began to propel her towards some of the tan leather benches, placed back to back in the main reception area. He said abruptly, 'Sit down. I'm going to phone up to the unit and see if they're ready for us.'

Lisle was thankful to feel the solid support of the bench under her. Her mouth was dry and she was shaking from head to foot. She found herself thinking with sudden mocking clarity that if she collapsed, at least it would be in the right place. She placed her folded hands on her knees, and sat staring at them, noticing almost detachedly the white knuckles, the strained grip of the slender fingers. She felt shattered. Incapable of assimilating what Jake had said, or rationalising it.

It seemed a very long time before Jake came back, but she knew that in reality it was only a few minutes. She looked up at his dark face, mentally bracing herself for more bad news, more shocks, but his cool, guarded expression gave nothing away.

'Sister says fifteen minutes. We'll go to the cafeteria and wait there.'

She didn't even think of protesting. She went with

him across the foyer to the lifts. An elderly man holding a bunch of flowers, a youth, barely out of his teens by the look of him, with his arm tenderly round the shoulders of a massively pregnant girl were already waiting. As the lift began its upward journey, Lisle found her gaze straying constantly to the young couple. The girl's left hand with its wide golden band lay protectively over her distended abdomen, and although she was clearly nervous, she was smiling up at her husband, her eyes bright with excitement and happiness.

Marriage, Lisle thought numbly, the ultimate partnership. Sharing a life, sharing a bed, conceiving a child in mutual passion, caring for it together. . . .

She glanced at Jake and found him watching her with such irony that her face was flooded with sudden, burning colour.

The cafeteria was a dazzle of bright lights, stainless steel, and red formica-topped tables with matching plastic seats. The coffee was surprisingly good and came in thick white institutional cups. Lisle refused anything to eat, but Jake bought a round of cheese sandwiches and ate them with every evidence of enjoyment. When he had finished, he pushed the plate away and looked at her.

'For Pete's sake stop staring at me as if you expect to be leapt upon at any moment,' he said. 'I promise you nothing could be further from my mind.'

'I wasn't!' Lisle denied indignantly. 'But you can't expect to—to spring things on me like that and expect me to take it in my stride.'

'I suppose not.' He gave her a long, considering glance. 'Well, Miss Bannerman, I think we'd better talk—or may I call you Lisle, seeing that we're practically engaged.'

'We are not engaged!' Lisle returned her cup to its saucer with a bang that even put that sturdy china at risk. 'I'd rather die!'

'Death before dishonour?' The firm lips curved in frank amusement. 'That's a curiously old-fashioned viewpoint.'

'I don't give a damn how old-fashioned it is,' she said shortly. 'Arranged marriages aren't exactly eighties-style either.'

'I don't think the Asian community among us would necessarily agree with you.' Jake's tone was deceptively mild. 'And they have our galloping divorce rate to back them up too. But that's by the way—what I really want to get across to you is that you're not to give Murray a blow-by-blow account of your true opinion of me, my manners, morals or anything else which occurs to you. This scheme of his to marry us to each other is dear to his heart, and you're not going to upset him by dismissing it out of hand.'

Lisle sat up very straight on the uncomfortable plastic chair. 'You're not suggesting that I should—go along with it?'

'Why not?' He gave her a level look. 'I'm prepared to—and I have just as little taste for you as you have for me, darling. But although you probably don't know it, Murray and I go a long way back. He was good to me when I was starting up, and gave me a lot of help and advice. I owe him, in other words, and I think you do too, lady, if your expensive flat, your pretty clothes and your sinecure at Harlow Bannerman are anything to go by, not to mention the unlimited expense account you and your brother have been running.'

'You have been busy,' Lisle commented, a bright spot of colour in each cheek.

The grey eyes hardened with contempt. 'It's time someone was, sweetheart, otherwise your private gravy train could come off the rails for good. Your grandfather has decided I'm the right man for the job, and my appointment as managing director will be confirmed by the board early next week.'

'Not if Gerard and I have anything to do with it,' she said furiously.

'Gerard will find himself isolated,' he said curtly. 'Perhaps you've forgotten that your voting shares in the company are under your grandfather's control until you're twenty-five, and he's already signed a proxy supporting my appointment.' He paused, then added with heavy emphasis, 'And he's selling me his own block of shares, so I won't just be running the company, trying to get it back on its feet again, I'll be controlling it too.'

Lisle drew a deep uneven breath. 'You—you took advantage of a sick old man. . . .'

He gave a derisive laugh. 'You'd better not let Murray hear you say that. He was in top form when he made our deal, and if you don't believe me ask Oliver Grayson.'

'That—Judas?'

He shrugged. 'On the contrary, I found him a good man. I think we're going to work well together.'

Lisle gripped the edge of the table, fighting for self-control. 'I don't believe a word of this. Grandfather would never sell his shares to you. He's always been adamant that they should remain in the family.'

And as far as he's concerned, they will,' he said calmly. 'But through his granddaughter and her husband, rather than his grandson as he'd intended. Gerard's unfailing record of unreliability and self-interest has caught up with him at last, I'm afraid. He knew that I was moving in, and he could have stayed and fought for his place in the sun. But no. As soon as he thought the danger was averted, he just cleared out, and that kind of failure in judgment can be fatal when you're trying to run a company in times like these.'

Lisle sat as if she had been turned to stone.

'Of course,' Jake went on, 'you might have been able to warn him, if you'd shown your face in the office for the past ten days, but your attendance record is one of

the poorest I've seen. Your department head is loyal to
the Bannerman name. He said you were working on a
promotion for the Salzburg Fair at home, but he didn't
speak with any real conviction. I suppose the poor guy
has never dared tell you that real public relations work
isn't merely acting as some kind of high class call-girl at
your brother's behest.'

She said hoarsely, 'You—bastard! How dare
you. . . .'

'I dare more than that,' he said flatly. 'I might not
even complain if it had all paid off—if the intimate
dinners for potential customers, the drunken thrashes at
your flat, the weekends on the boat had produced a full
order book. But even you must know that's not the
case. And yet you've a lovely face, and an enticing
body, so what went wrong? Perhaps your heart wasn't
in your work.'

Lisle felt sick with rage and shame. That he, or
anyone else, could think such things made her feel
utterly degraded, even though there was no reason for
it. She'd never been overwhelmed with enthusiasm for
acting as Gerard's hostess, but she played the role he
had chosen for her to the best of her ability, learning to
recognise the gleam in the eye which suggested that one
of the guests might be getting the wrong idea, and
distance herself with charm yet finality, because it was
Harlow Bannerman she was selling, and not, under any
circumstances, herself.

Yes, she had allowed Gerard to use the flat for
parties, but then as Harlow Bannerman were subsidising
the rent, she had felt she could hardly refuse. But she
had attended few of them herself, usually spending the
night with friends. And since Janie had moved in with
her, she had been able to use that as an excuse for
Gerard to go elsewhere, because there had been
disturbing indications that some of the entertainments
he gave were by no means as conventional or innocent
as he claimed.

Gerard had often laughed at her, complaining that she was a prude, and perhaps she was. Uneasily she recalled again the slapped face incident, and his subsequent fury, and there had been other occasions when his attitude had switched from amusement to exasperation, when he had exerted none too subtle pressure on her to 'relax', to be 'nicer' to certain clients. At times they had come close to quarrelling about it, but not seriously, because she couldn't believe that he meant it seriously.

But now suddenly she was no longer so sure. The fact that her own motives and behaviour had been so totally misunderstood was making her question Gerard's for the first time, and shed a new and disturbing light on his half grumbling, half amused accusations of prudishness.

She swallowed, steadying her hurried breathing. 'You have no right to say these things to me! What do you imagine my grandfather would think if he could hear you?'

'Murray hasn't been living in a vacuum for the past year or two,' he said. 'I don't think he suffers from many illusions, even about you. Love isn't always blind, you know. He probably wants to get you married off before some real disaster occurs. And as our paths hadn't crossed, I expect he hoped I wouldn't have heard of the reputation you were so busily garnering for yourself.'

Reputation, Lisle thought. If it wasn't so appalling, it would be almost funny. Because Gerard's accusations weren't so far from the truth. She couldn't explain it. It might be some kind of mental revulsion against her brother's inveterate womanising, it might be that she had never met a man who appealed to her sufficiently, or even because of some basic unsuspected flaw deep within her personality, but she was still, at twenty-three, a virgin.

The coffee was cold now, and bitter, but even so she

doubted if she could have lifted the cup without betraying how she was shaking. Jake was watching her closely—waiting for a confession, or some attempt at self-justification, she wondered furiously. Well, he'd wait for ever! she told herself, avoiding his intent gaze.

He said coolly, 'It's time we were going up to the ward. Sister was noncommittal but not particularly optimistic when I spoke to her, but he's conscious, and when he sees us together there'll be just one thing on his mind. Can I take it as read that you won't contradict me if I tell him we've just become engaged?'

She moistened dry lips. 'Will he believe it—as we've only just met?'

He shrugged one shoulder. 'If we were trying to convince him it was a love match, probably not. But as all three of us know the score, I think it will be a great relief to him that we're not wasting any time.'

'That's putting it mildly.' Lisle threaded the strap of her bag through her fingers. She managed an unsteady laugh. 'Just what am I being rushed into?'

'Well, certainly not marriage,' he drawled. 'I have no plans in that direction, and if I had they wouldn't include you, my dear Miss Bannerman. This is a pretence engagement, the sole purpose of which is to put your grandfather's mind at rest and reassure him about your future when he's no longer here to worry about you. So don't indulge in any fantasies that I've been swept away by your undoubted charms.' He stood up, and once again she was made unwillingly aware of his height, and the sheer domination of his personality. She had met a lot of successful men, but few of them had an iota of his undoubted physical attraction, and most of them by his age—mid-thirties, she judged— were already married and settled with families.

She walked silently beside him towards the lift, and still in silence rode up to the next floor where the intensive care unit was established.

It was like something out of a space odyssey, she thought uneasily, looking around her.

Sister in her sexless white gown was briskly reassuring. 'He's doing as well as can be expected, that's all I can say,' she told them in her office. She gave a rich chuckle. 'He's certainly a bonny fighter, but he's been getting himself dangerously over-excited. He's been giving my young nurses hell because they wouldn't bring him a telephone trolley—the very idea! I had to speak severely to him,' she added tranquilly.

Lisle managed a wavering smile in return. She was sitting in a chair facing Sister's desk, and Jake was perched on the arm of it. She was acutely conscious of the warmth of his body near hers, and it had been all she could do not to draw away when he sat down so close to her.

Jake said calmly, 'I hope the good news we have for him won't have an adverse effect.'

'Anything that will stop him worrying so much can only do good.' Sister paused. 'Am I to take it that congratulations are in order?'

With a shock, Lisle felt Jake's hand cover hers, then lift it to his lips. It was only the briefest caress, but her flesh felt as if it had been seared with a brand.

'You've guessed our secret, Sister,' Jake said softly. He looked down into Lisle's startled face, his lips smiling tenderly, but his grey eyes brilliant with mockery. 'As we're making no announcement yet, darling, we're going to have to try and hide our feelings for each other, at least in public.'

Through frozen lips, she managed, 'Yes.'

He bent towards her, and for one paralysed moment she thought he was going to kiss her on the mouth, and every nerve in her body reacted in tension. His touch on her hand had been ordeal enough, but to feel his lips on hers, caressing, exploring, parting, would be unendurable.

And he knew that quite well. Still holding her panic-stricken gaze with his, he drew back, his smile hardening sardonically. 'Shall we go and see Murray, my sweet?'

Sister bustled out and they were left to follow.

Lisle's lips moved. 'I don't think I can go through with this.'

Jake rose. 'Oh yes, you bloody well can.' He took her arms, hauling her bodily out of her seat. 'Everyone is capable of one selfless act, and this is going to be yours. Murray is going to rest with a tranquil mind tonight because he knows that what he cares most about in the world—Harlow Bannerman and you—are both in safe hands. So smile, darling. Pretend I'm an important customer or that poor devil who was pawing you when I arrived at the flat.'

She said dazedly, 'Who. . . .?' and saw the contempt flare again in his face.

He said half under his breath, 'No, I suppose you can't even remember his name. Heaven help any guy who falls hard for you, you little tease. Now look happy, and remember it's not for me, it's for Murray.'

But she was hard put to it to retain any semblance of cheerfulness when she stood by her grandfather's bed. She had never really understood what people meant when they talked about shadows of their former selves, but she knew now, because what seemed to be lying there was just a shadow of the man she loved. She sank her teeth into the softness of her inner lip as Murray Bannerman muttered something and opened his eyes. They had always been fiercely, intensely blue, but now that fire seemed muted, and his voice no more than a gruff whisper.

'Darling girl—so you came. And Jake. That's good. Good.'

She was amazed to hear how normal her voice sounded. 'Of course we're here. Don't try to talk. Everything's going to be fine.'

'Fine,' he repeated, and the faded eyes sought hers in a kind of entreaty. 'You and Jake.'

'Yes,' she said, her tone firming. 'He—he spoke to me about it, and although it was—rather a shock, I can see it would be best—for the company and for everyone, so I've agreed. I will marry him.'

The moment she'd spoken, she wished she hadn't used those particular words. At this moment, and in the presence of a man who could be dying, they savoured too closely of some kind of oath, the precursor to some future ritual where she and Jake would be made one, and she shivered suddenly.

Jake said, 'I'm going to take her away now, Murray, take her home, and let you get some rest. But we'll be back in the morning. Sleep well.'

Lisle felt the pressure of his hand on her arm, and turned away, fighting sudden blinding tears. He looked so frail, she thought in agony. What guarantee was there that he would see another morning, or know that they would return to share it with him?

She knew Jake was watching her, his dark brows drawn together in a frown of genuine concern, and as they walked to the lift, she fought a superhuman battle for control of her emotions and won. She hated him. She wanted nothing from him, especially his compassion.

They reached the ground floor and the doors opened silently, Jake standing aside to allow her to precede him.

Lisle said rapidly, 'There's a public telephone over there. Would you mind calling me a taxi, please.'

'There's no need for that,' he said brusquely. 'You're coming with me.'

'Oh, please!' Just for a moment her tone veered towards slight hysteria. 'How far do we have to carry this farce? Grandfather can't see us now, or know that we've gone our separate ways.'

His brows lifted. 'I was looking at the situation rather more practically. As we're both going to the Priory, one vehicle is surely quite sufficient.'

She looked at him stupidly, his words registering in some distant recess of her mind. 'You—you're staying at the Priory?'

'I told you I was staying there,' he said impatiently.

'I'd forgotten.' She gave herself a mental shake. 'Not that it matters. I can go to a hotel.'

'Like hell you can,' he said grimly. 'The Petersons are expecting you, and your old room has been prepared. What am I to tell them if you don't turn up? That your aversion to me is so great you can't face spending a night or two under the same roof?'

'You're the one with the instant solutions to everyone's problems,' she shot at him. 'You think of something.'

'I already have,' he returned. 'You're coming to the Priory with me, if it means I have to kick your charming backside every step of the way to the car.'

Lisle was going to say, 'You wouldn't dare,' but the words shrivelled in her throat as she realised there was very little if anything that Jake Allard wouldn't dare.

'Very wise,' he approved sardonically, reading her sudden silence with perfect accuracy. 'What a tragedy you weren't the man of the family. You have an infinitely better nose for danger than Gerard has. Now come on. Mrs Peterson promised she'd have supper waiting for us whatever time we got there.'

'Oh, I'm sure she's had her orders,' Lisle said scornfully. 'But don't you think you're being a little premature—coming on like the master of all you survey? You're not in the driving seat yet.'

'Perhaps not,' he said silkily. 'But when I am, my copper-haired vixen, you're going to be the first one to know.'

Lisle tossed her head angrily, and giving him a look in which frustrated rebellion and sheer venom were mixed about equally, went ahead of him into the darkness.

The Priory was only a few miles' drive away, and as

the car drew up on the gravelled sweep in front of the house, Lisle could see the massive double doors already opening to reveal Mrs Peterson's anxious figure in the stream of light from the hall.

'Oh, Miss Lisle!' Mrs Peterson's arms clasped her to her ample bosom. 'What a homecoming for you, my dear! But he'll get over it, don't you fret. He'll see us all out, I shouldn't wonder.'

Lisle smiled faintly as she kissed the plump cheek. 'Sister says he's a bonny fighter, Petey.'

'Hasn't he always been?' Mrs Peterson smiled at Jake. 'Good evening, sir, and thank you for bringing her. I've laid supper in the small dining room—it's cosier for two. I'll go and see to the soup while Peterson takes Miss Lisle's case up to her room.'

Lisle had been about to intervene, and say she couldn't eat a thing and would prefer to go straight to her room, but at the mention of soup, hunger betrayed her. She knew Petey's soups of old, made from bone and marrow stock and thick with fresh vegetables. Even Jake's presence across the table couldn't take the edge off such delights, she thought, realising how empty she was. No wonder, really. All she'd consumed since a light lunch had been a gin and tonic, a few canapés, and a cup of coffee at the hospital.

She washed and tidied her hair in the downstairs cloakroom, but left her face innocent of make-up. The last thing she wanted was Jake Allard to think she was employing any deliberate arts to attract him.

When she went into the drawing room, he was standing in front of the log fire, whisky and soda in hand. He said, 'May I get you something?'

'The perfect host,' she said on a jeering note. 'No, thanks.' Alcohol might help her to relax, she thought, but it was more important to keep all her wits about her.

He said, 'You have a very beautiful home.'

'Indeed I have,' she agreed. 'I'm surprised you

haven't persuaded Grandfather to sell it to you, along with everything else.'

Jake looked amused. 'I still might.'

'No, you won't,' she said with satisfaction. 'The Priory comes to me in Grandfather's will. Gerard gets his collection of pictures, the London flat and half the money. He showed us both when he drew the will up a few years ago.'

His brows rose in mocking acknowledgment. 'Very businesslike. And how reassuring to know exactly where you stand.'

'Indeed it is.' Lisle drew a deep breath. 'And I hope I don't have to inherit for at least ten years, if not twenty.'

The mockery was wiped away. He said soberly, 'I wouldn't count on it, Lisle.'

'Don't say that.' She shook her head in violent negation.

'Like you, I hope he lives for ever,' he said quietly. 'But we need to be realistic.'

She didn't want realism. She wanted the comfort and reassurance that her grandfather had represented since she was a small child. Without him, she thought confusedly, she would be totally bereft. If the worst did happen, she would leave London and come to live here in the house she loved. Her inheritance should ensure an adequate income, and she could live within it as long as she wasn't extravagant. She wouldn't really regret the loss of her job in the public relations department at Harlow Bannerman. She hadn't been a roaring success there, although she'd often felt she might have been if she'd only been given a chance. But nothing exacting, nothing that might stretch her mind and get the best out of her had ever come her way. The Bannerman name had always been there like a barrier. They had treated her like an unpredictable toddler, treading warily round her, and feeding her the odd unimportant sweet to keep her quiet. They had written her off as useless before she had even got there, she thought resentfully, and no one had ever bothered to discover what her capabilities were since.

She thought, without surprise, that it was probably from the PR department that the rumours about her sexual favours to customers had first emanated. She couldn't pretend that she was the flavour of the month with many of her colleagues. In fact, she heard herself described as 'Lady Muck' on more than one occasion when they thought she was out of the way. At the time, it had hurt, but she had made herself laugh it off. She was Lisle Bannerman, and nothing they could say could touch her.

Only now she knew differently. Mud had been thrown, and some of it had stuck as it had a habit of doing. The kind of things which had been said about her, the kind of implications which had been drawn from her behaviour made her feel unclean, and the thought that some of these vile rumours had found their way back to her grandfather and distressed him was intolerable. Yet he had never uttered one word of warning or reproach, she thought numbly.

Mrs Peterson's soup was everything she had remembered and more, and the cold roast chicken which followed was accompanied by a salad made infinitely more exciting by a selection of exotic ingredients. Jake asked for cheese to follow, but Lisle succumbed to the blatant temptation of a slice of home-made treacle tart, accompanied by thickly whipped cream.

Afterwards, Mrs Peterson deposited a tray of coffee in the drawing room and wished them goodnight.

Lisle poured the coffee, conscious of a feeling of awkwardness. Supper had been easier than she anticipated, with Mrs Peterson bustling in and out, making sure they were enjoying their food, and that they had everything they needed.

But now they had been left almost pointedly alone, and it made Lisle uneasy.

Jake on the other hand looked perfectly at ease. He had removed his jacket and slung it over the back of the big leather chesterfield and loosened his tie, and now he was leaning back, waiting for his coffee.

She handed him his cup, almost slopping it into the saucer in her haste, then got up to add another log to the already adequate fire, and fussily adjust one of the ornaments on the mantelpiece.

Jake gave her a bored look. 'Relax, for Pete's sake,' he told her. 'Rape is not imminent.'

'I never imagined it was,' she snapped, re-seating herself behind the coffee tray, and adding cream to her own cup.

Jake grinned suddenly. It made him look younger, and even more attractive, and Lisle decided she preferred him scowling. 'Then you should have,' he said. 'After all, we have the perfect set-up—a flickering fire, a beautiful girl, and damn all on television.'

In spite of loathing him, she felt her lips quiver. 'Aren't you the flatterer!'

'Not usually,' he said. He drank his coffee, and set the cup down on a table near his seat with a deliberation that she found slightly unnerving. He looked at her, and she thought confusedly that the lamplight had softened the colour of his eyes to silver. He held out his hand, and his voice was very gentle suddenly. 'Come here.'

And the shattering thing was that it would have been the easiest thing in the world to have got out of that chair and gone to him. It was unbelievable that she could feel that way, but she did. He was her enemy, and she hated him. He had insulted her and outraged all her feelings ever since he had walked into her life, and yet she remembered the way his mouth had scorched her hand, and knew that, in his arms, her whole body could turn to living flame.

And remembered too, just in time, that he thought she was the worst kind of tramp.

She said huskily, 'I'll see you in hell first.'

'Heaven might be more enjoyable,' he suggested, but she could hear the cynical note. He thought she was just playing hard to get, and that sooner rather than later she would let him make love to her.

She rose to her feet with a faint smile. 'Heaven?' she queried. 'Now you're flattering yourself, Mr Allard. I'll leave you to your fantasies, and go to bed. Alone.'

'What a waste,' he said softly. 'You wouldn't be disappointed. I'm sure my performance would reach the standard you've come to expect.'

'A personal guarantee,' she marvelled. 'Now there's a novelty! But I'm still not tempted. Goodnight.'

'One thing I would guarantee.' His voice was silky. 'That—come the dawn—at least you'd remember my bloody name. There's another novelty.'

Lisle walked to the door, nerves jumping at every step, in case he came after her. Because in spite of everything that had happened, she wasn't sure how she would react if he touched her, seriously wanted her. She hoped she would kick and bite and scratch to be free, behave like the vixen he'd called her, but she wasn't issuing any guarantees at all, and she knew she wouldn't feel safe until she was safely up in her room behind a door which, for the first time in her life, she would lock.

CHAPTER THREE

LISLE woke with a start in the pitch dark, remembering she had forgotten to telephone Gerard. Well, not forgotten, simply had no opportunity to do so without Jake guessing what she was up to. And she didn't want him to know. She wanted to be able to speak to Gerard in perfect privacy without Jake being able to overhear so much as a word.

Not for the first time, she sighed over Murray's intransigence on the subject of phone extensions in bedrooms. He thought they were immoral, a blatant temptation to people to be idle and run up enormous bills at the same time.

'A telephone's place is in the library,' he said. 'Let people make their calls at a civilised hour or not at all.'

The middle of the night was hardly a civilised time, Lisle thought ruefully, but it was all that was available.

She had fallen asleep at once, behind that safely locked door, so she hadn't heard Jake pass her room on his way to bed, but he would be sound asleep by now.

She sighed as she pushed back the covers and reached reluctantly for her robe. The first thing she would have to do was go to Gerard's own room, find his address book, and hope that Carla Foxton's Barbados villa was in it. If that address book ever fell into the wrong hands, it would probably be grounds for a dozen divorces, she thought as she padded softly across the carpet to the door. She stood for a moment on the landing, listening intently, but the house was at peace, not a light showing anywhere.

She found the address book in Gerard's bureau, and

slid it into the pocket of her robe, before beginning the journey downstairs.

The drawing room door was open when she reached the hall, and she could see the remaining embers of the logs still glowing red in the wide hearth. She wondered if Jake had remembered to set the spark guard in front of the fire, and decided she would see to it on the way back.

She closed the library door behind her noiselessly, and switched on the light, blinking for a few seconds at the sudden glare. Murray's big desk was set in the window recess, and the telephone was perched on one corner of it, trim scarlet lines looking strangely out of place among the antiques and rubbed leather which surrounded it.

After some initial difficulty in dialling, she managed to get through to the villa. The phone rang for a long time, and she was just about to give it up as a bad job, when the receiver was lifted and a woman's voice said, 'Yes?'

Lisle spoke politely, 'Good evening, Mrs Foxton. I wonder if I could speak to Gerard Bannerman.'

Silence crackled at her. Then, 'Who *is* this?'

'I'm his sister, Lisle. We met once, actually, at the Hargreaves' dinner party.'

'Oh, yes.' Carla Foxton's voice conveyed complete indifference. 'Well, what makes you think Gerard's here, Miss Bannerman?'

Lisle prayed for patience. 'As a matter of fact, I'm not sure where he is, Mrs Foxton. I hoped you might be able to help me. You see, there's rather a crisis here. My grandfather has had a severe heart attack, and I feel Gerard should come back immediately, for a number of reasons.' She paused, but there was no response from the other woman. 'So, if you do happen to know where he is, perhaps you could pass on a message for me.'

Another lengthy pause, then Carla Foxton said curtly, 'I'll see what I can do.' And rang off.

Lisle sighed as she replaced her own receiver more
slowly. It occurred to her that really she liked very few
of Gerard's women, and Carla Foxton probably least of
all. She was petite, black-haired and beautiful in a
voluptuous way which spoke of the Latin-American
blood in her recent ancestry, and Gerard had been
frankly besotted with her for several months. Carla was
some fifteen years younger than her wealthy indulgent
husband, and although Gerard was undoubtedly more
to her taste as a lover, their affair had been carried on
fairly discreetly. Carla much preferred to have the best
of both worlds, and was shrewd enough to ensure that
she did so. Lisle could understand her caution on the
phone, but not the lack of humanity she had displayed.

Dispiritedly, she walked to the door, and stepped out
into the hall, pausing as her hand reached for the switch to
plunge the library back into its former peaceful darkness.

'Walking in your sleep?' Jake asked.

She nearly screamed, her hand flying to her mouth
just in time to stifle the sound, so that it emerged
instead as a kind of strangled squeak.

He was lounging in the doorway to the drawing
room, his hand clasped round a tumbler of whisky. His
head was thrown back slightly, and the grey eyes were
narrowed as he looked at her.

Lisle said faintly, 'You—you startled me.'

'You startled me,' he returned pleasantly. 'When I
saw you go past the door, I thought for a moment you
were the resident ghost.' A faint appreciative smile
twisted the corners of his mouth. 'But if you were, of
course, I'd be able to see right through you, instead of
merely through that pretty nonsense you're wearing.'

Lisle realised with embarrassed dismay that, standing
in the strong light streaming from the room behind her,
she was providing him with a frank revelation of the
outline of her body through the thin nightdress and
robe. Hastily her hand moved to the switch again,
snapping it to the 'off' position.

'What are you doing down here?' she asked. Apart from a couple of extra buttons unfastened on his shirt, he was dressed exactly as when she had left him. It didn't seem as if he'd been to bed at all.

'Thinking,' he said. 'And drinking.' He held up the tumbler of whisky in a kind of mocking salute.

'You find alcohol aids your thought processes?'

'I find that sometimes it blocks them out altogether, which can be equally useful. May I ask, in return, what you're doing down here?'

'I—I couldn't sleep,' she said hurriedly. 'Worrying about Grandfather, I suppose.' She gestured towards the doorway behind her. 'I came down to get a book.'

He looked past her into the shadowed room with its tier upon tier of booklined shelves, then back to her empty hands. He began to laugh.

'But you couldn't find one. Or have you read them all before?'

She glared at him. 'Only I decided I'd rather have some hot milk instead. I was just going to get it.'

'Hot milk,' he said softly. 'How very girlish. May I recommend my own personal anodyne instead?'

'Whisky, I suppose.' Lisle pulled a small, jeering face.

'No,' he said. 'Not whisky.' And his eyes slid down her body from head to foot, assessing her in a slow deliberate sensual scrutiny, which left her oddly breathless and as vulnerable as if it had been his hands which had stripped her and left her naked beneath his hungry gaze.

She said on a little gasp, 'You're disgusting!'

'And you're a hypocrite,' he said derisively. 'You know what to expect when you flaunt yourself in front of a man with hardly a stitch on. And I'm not interested in your fables about books and hot milk either. There's a very good reason why we should both be roaming the house at two in the morning suffering from insomnia, and I'm sure I don't have to spell it out to you.'

She swallowed. 'It isn't what you think. . . .'

'As I've already told you, I've stopped thinking.' Jake put the glass down on the huge carved chest which stood against the wall next to him. 'I suggest you do the same. Just let your feelings take over. We may not like each other, Lisle, but I'm ready to bet any money that we have a common meeting ground just the same.'

He walked towards her, watching her, missing nothing, she thought desperately as she tried to steady her breathing, to control the hurry of her small breasts under the lace bodice of her nightdress.

He touched her face, his thumb caressing the soft curve of her cheek, his fingers discovering the delicacy of her jawline.

He said quietly, 'If it's any consolation, I never intended this to happen either.'

He took her quite gently into his arms, not kissing her, just holding her against the hard, lean length of him, and deep within her a pang of desire began a crescendo into real pain.

She was bewildered by it. It was too new to her experience, too sharp, and too urgent for her to know how to deal with it, although in some dim recess of her mind, something told her that she should pull away now while she still had some will to do so.

She knew by the pressure of Jake's body against hers that he was deeply and hotly aroused, and in the past she had always found that faintly disturbing, even alarming. Evidence, she had thought, of passions and emotions which seemed to pass her by, and which she had no wish to share.

Now, suddenly, it was exciting to know that she was wanted, and she evinced no kind of protest as his hands slid down her body to her slender hips, moulding her against him, because she knew that she wanted to be even closer still.

His hands moved on her without haste, his fingers stroking her body through the thin nightdress, the silky material creating a sweet erotic friction against her skin.

She was silent, eyes closed, within the circle of his arms, conscious only of this new sensual clamour in her blood, the uneven race of her pulse.

A few hours before, the thought of his kiss had filled her with tension, but now, when his hand gently cupped her throat, tipping her head back slightly so that his mouth could find hers, she reached for him with blind eagerness, like a parched flower thirsting for rain. His lips were warm and incredibly sensuous, demanding and winning an equally passionate response from her. Her hands locked behind his dark head, she felt her senses swim, her body melt in quivering eagerness.

Still kissing her, Jake slid an arm beneath her knees, lifting her bodily off the floor, then carried her across the hall to the warm shadows of the drawing room.

He knelt, lowering her gently to the huge fur rug spread in front of the fire, sliding the robe from her shoulders as he did so. The breath caught in her throat as she looked up at him, saw the grey eyes glittering suddenly, and hungrily intent. With the first sign of impatience he had shown, he pushed down the straps of her nightgown, baring the small rounded breasts, and Lisle gasped, lifting her hands instinctively to cover herself.

His fingers gripped her wrists, tugging her hands away. He said in a low voice, 'You're too beautiful to hide yourself. Let me look at you. I want to see every perfect inch.'

He freed her arms, and pulled the nightdress down from her body. In an agony of shyness, Lisle closed her eyes as she felt the soft silk slither away. There was little light in the room, but she'd never been naked in front of a man before, and it was a shattering experience for her, the cool reserve, which had always been her safeguard, broken in pieces.

Jake kissed her deeply and hotly, the aching thrust of his lips against hers exciting her feverishly. His hands closed on her breasts, his fingertips stroking their sensitive peaks, and she gave a little husky moan, her mind blanking out at a point between desire and panic.

He pulled away from her, and she knew by his movements, from the small telltale rustling noises, that he was taking his clothes off. When he took her in his arms again, the point of no return would have been reached, she knew, and it wouldn't be long after that before he was aware of her woeful lack of experience, and a long inward shudder gripped her as she wondered weakly what his reaction would be, recognising the fact that he could well be angry. After all, a willing woman was what he wanted, was expecting. A frightened virgin would make a poor substitute.

His lips brushed her eyelids. 'Falling asleep?' he sounded mocking. 'You can't be shy.'

Can't I? she thought, her body thrilling involuntarily at the touch of his skin against hers.

'Open your eyes,' he ordered huskily. 'You won't be turned to stone.' His hand moved down her body, moulding and tracing every supple fluent line as if he was learning her by heart, and she swallowed, her breath thickening as his fingers lingered intimately on her thigh, their subtle pressure luring her to a new and devastating submission. He was kissing her body, his mouth moving slowly and pleasurably on her skin, his head dark as night against her whiteness. She was dissolving in waves of delight, poised on the edge of yielding totally, letting those diabolically experienced hands explore her in any way he wished.

The sudden violent thresh of the telephone bell was like the shock of an electric current, a whiplash across her senses. Jake swore, levering himself away from her, the swift dark anger in his face turning to ruefulness as he looked down at her.

'I'll have to answer that before the Petersons do.'

Dry-mouthed, Lisle said, 'Their room is in another wing. They won't hear. . . .'

He drew a finger over her lips, silencing her. 'You realise that it might be the hospital,' he said quietly, and was gone.

She put her hands over her eyes, wanting to die of shame. No, she thought, it hadn't occurred to her, because she'd been lost to all sense of reality, aware only of the devastation of this physical arousal he had created in her.

She sat up shivering, feeling bleak and cold, reaching for her crumpled nightdress and dragging it over her head, guilt and shame warring inside her.

How could she have behaved like this? she wondered desperately. In a matter of hours after their first meeting, Jake had made her act like the slut he believed her to be, and she would never forgive herself. Grandfather could be dying, and she had let a man she didn't even like strip and touch her and kiss her, without lifting a finger to stop him.

She huddled on her robe, and sat hugging her knees, staring with empty eyes at the charred logs in the wide grate as she waited for Jake to come back.

He said from the doorway, 'It's Gerard. Returning the call you made to him earlier.'

Lisle got up stiffly, not daring to look at him, and fled to the library.

'What's he doing there?' Gerard demanded instantly, without even the preamble of a greeting.

'Taking over the company, unless you can stop him. What do you think?' Lisle retorted.

He cursed viciously. 'I'll get the next plane out. Thank goodness Carla gave me your message, although it was touch and go,' he added on a unmistakable note of satisfaction. 'I don't think she altogether believed you're my sister. She was actually jealous!'

Lisle felt a little sick. 'I'm not really interested in the emotional games you and your women friends play,' she said tautly. 'Aren't you going to ask about Grandfather?'

'Just how sick is he?' he asked sharply. 'What guarantee is there that I'm going to be in time?'

'None at all,' Lisle's voice was crisp. 'Thanks for caring.'

He sighed. 'Oh, I didn't mean it like that, sweetie. I'm just in a bit of a state, that's all. I wasn't expecting this—any of it.'

'Nor was I.' Lisle's tone was still short. 'Can I tell Grandfather that you're on your way when we go and see him tomorrow—today?' she corrected herself hurriedly.

'Of course,' Gerard said slowly. 'Lisle—when you said "we" . . .'

'That's exactly what I meant.' She was aware that Jake was standing in the doorway watching her, buttoning his shirt and stuffing it into the waistband of his slacks as he did so.

'You keep that bastard away from Grandfather, do you hear!' Gerard snapped with angry emphasis.

Lisle smiled bitterly. 'If only it was as simple as that. Just get here as soon as you can.' She put the receiver back on the rest and turned to face Jake with spurious calm.

He looked back at her with an angry disgust he did not bother to conceal. 'I'd fogotten the telephone was in the library,' he said half to himself. 'That's why you were in there, of course, summoning the cavalry to come galloping to the rescue.' His mouth curled. 'But you picked up the cue I gave you quite brilliantly, darling. When the world of public relations has nothing more to offer you, which should be soon, you might try the stage. A certain class of production, of course. All that romantic trembling, the modestly averted eyes as you take your clothes off, would be a riot with the dirty raincoat brigade.'

She shrugged elaborately, not daring to meet his hostile gaze directly. 'It left you cold, naturally.'

'Unfortunately, no,' he said. 'Dressed, your body makes all kinds of promises which are more than fulfilled when your clothes are off. I'd be a fool and a liar if I even attempted to deny it. Tell me something, beauty. Are there any lengths you won't go to in order to help that no-good brother of yours?'

The words stung, but she made herself smile. 'Why, yes,' she said softly, 'I wouldn't go to bed with you, Mr Allard—I'm not that good an actress, I'm afraid.'

For a long violent moment he stared at her, a dark smudge of furious colour along his cheekbones, then he turned and left the room.

Lisle sagged with relief, leaning back against the desk, letting its solid lines support her while she recovered her composure. Janie's words of warning came filtering back into her mind, and she realised wryly that she had undoubtedly succeeded in turning Jake Allard from an uncertain friend into a bad enemy, with all which that implied, and it was not a comfortable sensation. But at least it meant she would not have to be constantly fighting him off, she tried to tell herself, and shivered weakly as she remembered the passionate expertise of the lips and hands which had caressed her to the point of madness.

If she thought she had achieved any kind of victory, she was fooling herself, she realised unhappily. The real battle she would have to fight would be against herself, and the unexpected depths of sensuality in her own nature which had been awakened but not satisfied.

As she moved wearily to the door, she knew she had embarked on a voyage of self-discovery that she would far sooner never have begun.

She felt like death when Mrs Peterson came in with her breakfast tray next morning. The housekeeper clucked disapprovingly over her wan face and deeply shadowed eyes, and then passed on the message that Mr Allard suggested they leave for the hospital in an hour's time.

'He rang up earlier, and they said your grandfather

had had a good night,' she added with evident
satisfaction.

Lisle managed a few sips of orange juice, and poured
herself a cup of strong black coffee, but the sight of
food made her stomach close up in rejection. Mrs
Peterson's words had been a potent reminder that only
too soon she would have to go downstairs and face
Jake in the cold light of day, with the memory of
everything that had happened the previous night lying
between them like a stone.

She had hoped against hope that he might not be
there, that he might have decided to move into a hotel,
but she supposed she should have known better. It
would be war to the knife between them now, and he
wouldn't be the first to back away.

She bathed quickly, and took a certain amount of
care over her choice of clothes, picking a suit with a
softly bloused jacket made from fine needlecord in a
dark green shade. She brushed her copper hair and
twisted it back severely from her face into a french
pleat, putting tiny emerald studs into the exposed lobes
of her ears. Eyeing herself critically, she decided her
appearance gave her just the touch of formality she had
wanted to convey.

She waited until the hour Jake had specified had
elapsed however before she went downstairs. The
drawing room door was tight shut and she could hear the
sound of a vacuum cleaner being vigorously used behind
it, signifying that the woman from the village who helped
Mrs Peterson with the housework had duly arrived.

She stood irresolutely in the hall, wondering where
Jake was, then heard him speaking in the library and
realised that he was on the phone. She heard the words
'meeting next week' and 'could be vital' and realised
that he was discussing Harlow Bannerman. She knew
she ought to move away from the library door and give
him some privacy, but she didn't. After all, he had
barged in last night while she was talking to Gerard.

She heard him say, 'And there's been another, unexpected development, but I'll talk to you about that when I see you,' and flushed, as she wondered whether he meant Murray's insistence on their becoming engaged. She didn't hear the receiver go down, and the next thing she knew the door had opened wide and Jake was watching her sardonically.

'Hear anything instructive?' he asked derisively.

Lisle made herself meet his gaze. 'I think I arrived too late.'

'Better luck next time,' he said shortly. 'Can you manage shorthand? If not, one of those little pocket tape recorders should be useful.'

'Thanks for the tip. Of course Harlow Bannerman has never gone in for industrial espionage, but I'm sure you're an expert.'

'I wouldn't go that far,' he drawled. 'But if a commodity's for sale, then I'm generally in the market, as you discovered for yourself last night. Now, shall we go?'

She nodded coolly.

Murray was watching the door eagerly when they came in, and a satisfied smile crossed his face when he saw Jake's hand cupped protectively under Lisle's arm.

'Ready to play your part—darling?' he had asked her sneeringly as they came along the corridor.

Now, she looked at Murray and smiled radiantly. 'You look wonderful!' She crossed to the bed and kissed him.

'I feel better,' he said. 'And I'm sick of this damned place already.'

'You have to be patient.' Lisle seated herself beside the bed, and clasped his hand.

'Hm,' he grunted. 'At my age, I can't afford patience.' He gave her one of his gimlet glances. 'Have you settled your wedding day yet?'

She tensed incredulously, then forced herself to give a little laugh. '*Darling*, we—we've only just met! You have to give us a chance—well, to get to know each other a little.'

'I want the date settled,' Murray said flatly. 'It will give me something to look forward to—something to aim for.'

Lisle seized the opportunity. 'Gerard's flying home today.'

'Obliging of him,' her grandfather growled. 'Where the devil's he been anyway?'

'Just—staying with friends abroad.' Lisle studiously avoided the satirical look Jake sent her. 'He can't wait to see you.'

Murray muttered something inaudible and relapsed into silence, but he didn't look particularly pleased, and Lisle's heart sank as she watched him covertly from beneath her lashes. She began to chat about trivialities, relating incidents that had occurred over the past few weeks which might amuse him. He smiled and interjected the occasional comment, but she knew him well enough to realise that his mind was really elsewhere, and she wasn't really surprised when he dispatched her to Sister's office with an abrupt request to find out when he would be allowed home.

It was obvious that he wanted a private word with Jake, and it galled her not to know what was being said, to know that a man who was a comparative stranger to them all was receiving Murray's confidences instead of his own family.

His repressive attitude towards Gerard had alarmed her too. She hadn't realised how far the relationship between them must have deteriorated, although the very fact of his secret negotiations with Jake Allard should have been sufficient warning, she was forced to acknowledge.

If he had been satisfied with Gerard, had intended him ultimately to succeed him as chairman of the company, then they would never have taken place, she knew.

She wondered if Gerard realised the depths of Murray's disillusionment with him, and whether, when he did arrive, he would be able to recoup any of the ground he had lost.

Or even if Jake would allow that to happen, she thought ruefully. Family disloyalty was abhorrent to her, but she had to admit that Jake would have the edge over Gerard every time if it came to an open battle between them as seemed likely. He was hard, determined and already successful, and it was sheer bad luck that it was Murray Bannerman's help and advice which had started him on the road to that success.

Gerard, she thought wistfully, had had exactly the same advantages. Why hadn't he achieved as much?

Day Sister was an older woman, and rather more reserved. She heard Lisle out in a forbidding silence, and said merely that Mr Bannerman would be undergoing more tests and continuing to receive treatment for his condition. There was no possibility of his leaving hospital at the moment, and she hoped Miss Bannerman would be able to convince him of this, and not permit his current treatment to be undermined by useless fretting.

'He is in the best place, and receiving the best of attention,' Sister added austerely, folding her lips, and reaching for one of the files on her desk so as to signify that the interview was at an end.

Lisle walked slowly back to Murray's room. Jake came to meet her.

'The specialist's on his way, and we're clearly *de trop*, so I told him we'd be back this evening,' he said. 'How did you make out with Sister?'

'Not too well,' she admitted reluctantly, and told him what had transpired.

He smiled faintly. 'Murray said she was a dragon lady. I've just told him to behave himself, if he wants to avoid a lengthy stay here.'

She wondered what else they had discussed, but Jake

did not seem prepared to tell her, and she was damned if she was going to ask him. He hardly addressed more than two words to her on the way back to the Priory, and about half an hour later she heard him drive off, and learned from Mrs Peterson that he had gone up to Town and wouldn't be back before evening.

Lisle digested this with growing anger. Why hadn't he told her he was planning to go to London? There was nothing to do here but hang round the house all day alone, and she didn't feel inclined to do that. On an impulse, she phoned Harlow Bannerman and asked to be put through to Oliver Grayson's office.

'Lisle?' He sounded sharply concerned. 'What is it? Is Murray all right?'

'He seems fine,' she returned lightly. 'He thinks if he declares war on the nursing staff, they'll discharge him.'

He laughed, but there was a strained note in his voice. 'That sounds like the Murray of old. We were all—deeply upset—deeply disturbed to hear about him, Lisle. If there's anything I can do, you have only to let me know, my dear.'

She took a breath. 'As a matter of fact there is something, Oliver. I was thinking of getting a train up to do some shopping, and wondered if you'd like to give me lunch?'

'I should be delighted,' he said gallantly, but again she thought she detected a slight reserve in his tone. 'Perhaps if you're shopping, it might be better if we met at the restaurant. Shall we say the Chanticleer at one? I'll get my secretary to book a table.'

'Marvellous,' she approved, smiling. 'It's been ages since we saw each other—or really talked,' she added deliberately.

'So it is.' His voice lightened perceptibly. 'Until one o'clock, then.'

Lisle replaced the receiver thoughtfully. Oliver Grayson had been divorced for several years, and when she had first gone to work at Harlow Bannerman she had been well aware that he fancied her, although she had never been tempted to encourage him particularly. However, she had gone out to dinner with him, and to the theatre on odd occasions, and spent a pleasant evening, and Oliver had never ventured further than a chaste kiss on her cheek which had suited her very well.

She didn't change again, but merely brushed her hair into its usual casual waves on to her shoulders, and added some extra sparkle to her eyes, cheeks and lips.

Oliver was already waiting for her in the small cocktail bar which adjoined the restaurant when she arrived punctually at one. He rose smiling as soon as he saw her.

'Lisle, you look wonderful as ever!' He ushered her solicitously into her seat, and beckoned a waiter. 'What would you like to drink?'

'I think—a dry Martini.' Lisle adjusted her skirt as she sat down, aware of the covert glance Oliver stole at her legs. He was immaculate as ever in his navy blue pinstripe suit, his fair hair beginning to thin at the temples. He was good-looking in a rather pale way, and although he was by no means the 'bloodless cretin' that he was stigmatised by Gerard, Lisle had to admit that he was not a particularly dominating personality.

'Well, how are you, Lisle?' he asked as the drinks were served. 'We don't seem to see a great deal of you these days.'

'I think perhaps I should come in more often,' she said drily, and he looked faintly startled.

'I—I didn't mean that as a criticism, you know. After all, it isn't really my department, and besides——' he stopped abruptly, looking embarrassed.

'Besides, it isn't a real job, but just something which was dreamed up to keep me out of mischief where I could do no harm,' Lisle finished for him, rather wearily. 'I am aware of these things, Oliver.'

He looked embarrassed still. 'I suppose—yes, you

must be. Although I'm sure you more than justify whatever salary you're paid.'

'Well, thank you, Oliver,' she said evenly. 'Can I count on your support next week if the question of my future with the company is raised by Mr Allard?'

Oliver, who was helping himself to cashew nuts, nearly choked.

'Or wasn't I supposed to know?' she went on sweetly. 'I'm disappointed in you, Oliver. I thought an old friend would have warned me what was in the wind. As I say, I should come into the office more often.'

Another waiter approached with menus, and Oliver took refuge behind his, murmuring something about 'delicate stage in negotiations' and 'any announcement being premature'. Phrases Lisle seemed to remember from the newspaper stories about Harlow Bannerman being acquired by Allard International only a few weeks earlier.

The Chanticleer was a gourmet eating hole, specialising in chicken dishes as its name suggested, but Lisle ordered a rare fillet steak and a salad, knowing that Oliver would be disconcerted by her choice as he cared deeply about food, and liked to have long discussions with the head waiter and the wine waiter to produce a perfectly balanced meal. Perversely, she wanted to annoy him, and was rewarded by the briefly pained look which crossed his features as he gave the order.

He said, 'Now tell me about Murray. It was a terrible shock to us all, as you can imagine. He semed so well again—so hopeful.'

'That's an odd word to use.' Lisle raised her eyebrows.

'But appropriate.' Oliver gave a short sigh. 'I'm not sure if you know how things stand with the company, Lisle, but they're not good, and haven't been for some time. We've been up against stiff competition, and we haven't been winning as much of our share of the market as we should have done, and that's worrying even when there isn't a recession, muddying the water, and throwing everything into confusion. Ally our recent performance to severe economic depression, and the sum adds up to disaster. Our research section has come up with the goods, but we need new investment in order to produce them. Allard International is prepared to supply that.'

Lisle smiled tightly. 'He made us an offer we couldn't refuse. I see.' She drank some of her Martini. 'Jake Allard told me you were on his side, but I didn't believe him.'

Oliver looked uncomfortable. 'It's hardly a question of sides, my dear . . .'

'Isn't it?' She gave him a direct look. 'You worked for my grandfather, Oliver, and for my father. You've always claimed to have loved them both. I thought at least Harlow Bannerman could count on your loyalty.'

He shifted restlessly. 'Loyalty doesn't come into it, Lisle, as I'm trying to make plain to you. It's a simple question of economic expediency. We need Allard International—and Jake Allard too—or we're going to go under.'

'And when we're finally absorbed into his empire, what then?' Lisle stared at him. 'Do you want the Bannerman name to disappear? For Murray to live to see everything he's struggled for vanish—down that shark's throat?' she added violently, and Oliver looked shocked.

'My dear girl, I know you're having a wretched time, but you must calm yourself. It isn't the end of the world, believe me. And I'm sure the Bannerman name will be retained in some context at least. Your grandfather was determined about that. After all,' he added with a faint smile, 'he kept his former partner's name, even though Anthony Harlow was only with the company for a few years before his death. He's got some scheme to keep the Bannerman name alive, I know that, and I'm sure Jake Allard will agree to it. It's a fine name, and there's a lot of goodwill attached to it, after all.'

'Yes.' Her fingers played with the stem of her glass, thinking of the exact method her grandfather had chosen to perpetuate the family name in the company. She said with a small grimace, 'Oliver, I'm so scared.'

It was the truth, although she would probably have said it anyway. She had arranged this lunch, intending to try and win Oliver over, away from his new-found allegiance to Jake Allard, to try and obtain, although she wasn't sure how, some kind of breathing space for Gerard to re-establish himself as his grandfather's heir, to try and beat Jake Allard at his own game.

It had seemed a reasonable notion back at the Priory, where there were all the memories of the previous night to torment her, and give shape and purpose to her anger. But here in London, in the bright cold light of day, the idea of flirting with Oliver in order to thwart Jake Allard in some way she had yet to establish suddenly seemed not quite so harmless. In fact, it could even be positively dangerous, quite apart from the morality of it.

Jake's raw condemnation of her had made her very angry, because she knew that basically she was innocent, and had not been given a chance to speak in her own defence. And there was no real reason why his arrogant and twisted opinion of her should matter to her anyway. Yet to deliberately set out to entice Oliver Grayson into forming some kind of alliance against Allard International was in some way to traverse the abyss she had always prided herself on avoiding.

Oliver was a gentleman, but he was also a man of the world, and she had no reason to believe he'd been leading a celibate life since his divorce, and if she was going to win him it wouldn't be with the promise of continuing kisses on the cheek, she thought miserably.

Of course, he might ask her to marry him. She had

half expected it at one time, but guessed he had been deterred by the fact that he was twenty years older than herself, and that Murray Bannerman had old-fashioned ideas about divorce and re-marriage.

'My poor love!' His voice was full of concern. His hand covered one of hers and his arm slid along the back of the velvet banquette they were occupying. Lisle allowed herself to relax slightly against him, but not sufficiently to embarrass him in public, while she thought clinically about being married to Oliver. His touch was certainly comforting, but it awoke no secret fires deep within her. She tried to imagine a situation where she would welcome Oliver's hands on hers without the excuse of comfort, and failed. 'What are you scared of?'

'Jake Allard,' she said with a small crooked smile. 'What else?'

'But he can't harm you, and anyway, why should he want to?' Oliver said soothingly. 'You're Murray's granddaughter. You have nothing to fear.'

She could see his point. Since birth, she had been cushioned against the realities of life by money and security and unquestioning affection. And that same affection would see to it that she was well provided for when her grandfather was no longer there to care for her.

'No, I suppose I haven't,' she said. 'Yet there was a story I always hated when I was a child—the one about the Three Little Pigs. I have this—obsession that Jake Allard is going to huff and puff and blow my house down.' She laughed. 'Ridiculous, isn't it?'

She felt Oliver stiffen, and looked at him with incredulity in her eyes, wondering if her words had touched some nerve—if he knew something that she didn't—and saw that he was looking over her shoulder towards the door.

She turned to see what had attracted his attention and felt as if all the breath had been knocked out of her body in one choking gasp.

Jake had just walked into the bar and was standing, looking casually around, and beside him, her arm twined with evident possession through his, was one of the most beautiful girls Lisle had ever seen.

CHAPTER FOUR

'TALK of the devil,' Oliver muttered. 'We shouldn't have come to such a popular place.'

Lisle moved her lips, and a sound that might have been 'No' emerged.

She had turned away immediately, praying that he wouldn't see her, although it didn't seem likely. She was wearing the same clothes as she had been when they had gone to the hospital—although she had noticed that he had found time to change into yet another dark, expensive suit—and she hadn't even a scarf to cover her hair, let alone a bag to put over her head, she thought, grinding her teeth.

'It's all right,' said Oliver. 'They've gone straight through to the restaurant. I don't think he saw us. Who was that amazing creature he was with? Her face seemed familiar.'

'A model—I think.' Lisle had recognised her too, although she knew they had never met.

'Well, at least it proves he's human.' Oliver was smiling, but she thought she could detect a trace of envy in his words. He lowered his voice. 'Look, they know me here, and if you'd rather cancel our table—try somewhere else, I'm sure I can square it.'

'Certainly not.' Lisle gave him a level look. 'Unless you'd rather he didn't see us together.'

'The thought never crossed my mind,' he said helplessly after a pause. 'Lisle, you surely don't think. . . .'

'No, of course not.' She relented, squeezing his hand. 'You see the effect he has on me, Oliver? One glimpse, and I start griping! And I think our table's ready.'

A deferential waiter led them into the restaurant. It

was a large room, irregularly shaped, and most of the smaller tables were sited round the walls, and shielded from their neighbours by an elaborate framework of trellises and flowering plants. As they were conducted towards one of these alcoves, Lisle did her best not to look and see where Jake was sitting, but she knew all the same, just as if she had some private radar system.

The mushrooms which comprised their first course were delicious, but, although she responded to Oliver's enthusiasm for them with little appreciative noises, she barely tasted them. Her stomach was churning in an agony of nervousness, and she ate whatever was put on her plate and swallowed the wine poured into her glass without any real consciousness of what she was doing. And at the same time, she carried on a conversation with Oliver, casting caution to the winds as she looked at him, smiling, using her lashes, even the curve of her body as she leaned towards him to provoke him. She'd done it all before, to a lesser extent, at Gerard's instigation, and she recognised the frankly dazed expression in Oliver's eyes as he began to read her signals. There was a point, she knew, at which harmless flirtation could become sexual teasing, and this was something she tried to avoid. But not today. Today she felt reckless, lit from within by a force she did not recognise, and dared not examine too closely.

At last Oliver said rather hoarsely, 'Shall we have coffee here, or perhaps go back to my place?'

Well, she'd asked for it, and now the decision was hers, and for the life of her, she didn't know what to say to him. A flat refusal, and he would feel cheated, but if she agreed. . . . A wave of self-disgust swept over her as her imagination swept her forward an hour—two hours in time. She swallowed, said, 'Oliver—I. . . .' and then stopped short, realising they were not alone.

Jake looked down at her, her dark face cynical as he appraised her.

'Life in the country soon palled,' he remarked softly, then turned to her companion. 'Grayson, I need a word with you fairly urgently. I presume you'll be going straight back to the office from here?'

Oliver recovered well. 'Of course—once I've seen Lisle safely on her way.'

'It's all right,' she intervened hastily. 'I can get a taxi to the station.' She pulled back her cuff to look at her watch. 'In fact I didn't realise how late it was getting—I should really be going now.'

'I'll tell the doorman to get you a cab,' said Jake, and turned away.

Oliver looked frankly crestfallen, as he signed the bill, and Lisle felt wretchedly guilty. She said, trying to smile, 'It was a wonderful lunch, Oliver. I'm—sorry it had to end so soon.'

'So am I.' He squeezed her hand conspiratorially as they walked to the door. 'I'll ring you.'

'I'll look forward to it,' she lied. When she came out of the cloakroom, she found Oliver standing talking to Jake and his companion, and she made herself walk towards them very slowly and carefully in case the wine she had drunk, added to her inner tensions, betrayed her, and she fell over her own feet.

Jake's brief smile barely touched his lips, and went nowhere near the cold grey eyes as he looked at her. 'May I introduce Cindy Leighton?'

'How do you do?' Lisle shook hands as he swiftly completed the introduction.

Seen close to, Cindy Leighton was almost incredibly good-looking, but there was a faintly predatory light in the huge blue eyes as she looked at Lisle. She had no compunction either about touching Jake, stroking his sleeve, twining her fingers round his, even while they were standing in so public a place as a restaurant foyer. Establishing ownership, Lisle thought wryly. In spite of her anger, and other confused emotions, she was irresistibly reminded of a scene from a John Wayne movie where a minor character had been moved to make the immortal protest, 'I'll thank you to unhand my fee-anc-ay.' She imagined saying it, and seeing those blue eyes glazing over in disbelief, and the perfectly moulded lips gaping unprettily.

'I'm not nice,' she decided with a certain satisfaction.

Oliver was saying, '*Now* I know where I've seen you before. You've been in all the papers. You're going to play the lead in a big film in the States.'

Cindy Leighton smiled, displaying perfect teeth, and Lisle wondered, purely academically, how much time and money it would take to restore that perfection, should some accident befall.

'I've been incredibly lucky,' she murmured modestly. 'There was really fierce competition for the part. I can't imagine why they chose me.'

'Novelty value,' Lisle heard herself suggest.

'Of course British actresses have always been very big in the States,' Cindy went on, treating the last remark as unsaid. 'I just hope I live up to everyone's expectations of me.' She made a little rueful face which she probably practised in front of her mirror every morning. 'It's the most wonderful chance, but——' she sent a laughing look at Jake in which she also managed to combine wry regret, and unequivocal sexual desire. One of her audition pieces? Lisle wondered. 'It would have to happen just now. Frankly, I feel torn in half.'

Well, guess who won't want the half that talks, the malicious stranger currently inhabiting Lisle's brain muttered, and she could only be thankful that it wasn't aloud. She was shocked at herself. Generally, she liked her own sex. She'd never regarded other women as rivals or potential enemies, even though she didn't go along with total sisterhood either. She thought, 'I must be drunk', and giggled.

Jake said icily, 'I think your taxi's arrived.'

Oliver's arm was round her, protective but oddly alien. The air in the street felt very cold after the centrally heated atmosphere of the restaurant, shocking her into sudden sobriety. Tentatively, she offered Oliver her cheek, but his eyes were fixed greedily on her mouth, and she knew she wasn't going to get away with it this time. As she endured the eager cling of his lips, she wondered if Jake was watching. She kept her mouth clamped shut and after what seemed an age he let her go, evidently disappointed by her lack of response. As he had every right to be, she thought wearily as she let him put her in the taxi, and close the door. After all, she'd been promising him heaven and earth all through that abominable meal.

She had a splitting headache by the time she reached the station, and she had half an hour to wait for her train, which didn't help. She drank a cup of coffee she didn't particularly want in the buffet, and told herself she should be glad she wasn't at Oliver's flat discovering how his technique differed from Jake's.

She could hardly believe that it was herself, Lisle Bannerman, who was thinking these things, even admitting them as possibilities. It was totally out of character. But then perhaps everyone reacted like that when their world was pushed sideways suddenly. Ever since Jake Allard had walked into her life the previous evening, she had lost touch with herself in some strange way. The real Lisle would never have behaved as she had done, she thought restlessly.

She dozed a little on the train, aware of swift and disturbing dreams which she was glad she could not remember too clearly.

There was no dread message from the hospital waiting when she got back to the Priory, and she whispered a silent prayer of thankfulness as she went up to her room. She changed into a pair of elderly denims, topping them with a navy Guernsey sweater, and scooped her hair back, confining it with an elastic band at the nape of her neck.

The secondhand Mini she used as a runabout when

she was in the country was kept in one of the outhouses off the old stableyard, and she backed it out with care across the yard to the tap in the corner. It had started at first try, which was a good sign, and Peterson had assured her that he had had it serviced only recently. But it could do with some cosmetic treatment, she thought, coupling up the hose to the tap.

Washing cars was by no means her favourite chore, but gradually, in the crisp autumnal air, the hard exercise of hosing down, drying and polishing began to restore her equilibrium. She even began to hum a tune as she worked.

She would drive herself to the hospital tonight, she thought. Establish her independence. She grimaced as she realised that Murray would be expecting her to arrive with Jake, but she would think of some excuse why they were not together, then, gradually, as his health improved she would get him to accept the fact that the marriage plan he cherished was unworkable.

'We don't even like each other,' she would have to tell him eventually. 'And he has a glamorous blonde lady hanging on his every word, and any other part of him she can reach, while I—I'm going to marry Oliver Grayson.'

She pronounced the last few words with less conviction, even in her head, although she had little doubt she could make it happen if she really wanted to. But did she want to? She'd known Oliver for a long time—nearly all her life, in fact. She remembered Hilary his ex-wife too. They had met and married at university, from what she could recall, and Hilary had been some kind of flower child. She had found adapting to the role of executive wife rather hard to take from all accounts, and eventually she had just stopped trying and gone off with the tutor of her pottery class to try self-sufficiency in Wales.

Lisle thought Oliver still heard from her occasionally. Certainly he seemed to harbour no bitterness towards her, and there were no children for them to squabble over.

She thought Oliver would probably have made quite a nice father, and in fact could still do so. If he remarried, he might well want to start a family.

She bit her lip hard. She must stop casting Oliver in these roles, she thought. He was attractive and reliable and certainly one of the cornerstones of Harlow Bannerman, but she had never considered him in the light of a future husband before, or anyone else either, if it came to that.

She was letting Murray's ridiculous suggestion completely unnerve her, and it wasn't necessary. The engagement was only a fake, and there would be no marriage. After all, what had Jake said? *'I have just as little taste for you as you have for me.'* That was her safeguard.

But after last night, just how safe was it?

He had wanted her badly, and she had been going quietly crazy in his arms when Gerard's call had interrupted them, and she found herself wondering how she would have felt if there had been no phone call, and she had let him make love to her there on the rug, and perhaps later up in his room. She pushed the thought resolutely away. There was no profit in that kind of speculation.

The car positively gleamed when she had finished, and she felt proud of her handiwork as she re-coiled the hose, and put the wax polish and the cloths back in the garage. Her grandfather's Jaguar gleamed in the shadows, and she wondered with a pang whether Murray would ever sit behind the wheel again.

She was passing through the hall on her way to the stairs when she heard Jake's car pull up. She took the stairs two at a time. She felt windblown and grimy after her exertions, and she didn't want to face him. At least not yet. Mrs Peterson was serving dinner before they were due to go to the hospital, and during the meal she would try and persuade him that there was nothing he could usefully achieve by remaining at the Priory.

It wasn't even as if she was going to be alone there with the Petersons, because Gerard would be arriving that evening, which was another excellent reason for Jake to return to London.

She pulled off her sweater, tossed it on the bed and walked into the bathroom to wash. When she returned to her bedroom a few moments later, it was to find Jake lounging on the end of her bed, waiting for her.

'Get out of here!' she snapped furiously, snatching up the guernsey and holding it in front of her.

He looked her over, the firm mouth mocking, the dark brows lifted in exaggerated surprise, his gaze lingering pointedly on her tied-back hair, the patched jeans, and the well-scrubbed face.

'What's the new image?' he drawled. 'A regression to adolescence?'

'What am I supposed to wear to wash a car?' she snapped defensively. 'Ermine and pearls? And perhaps next time you'd knock at my door, instead of just barging in!'

'I did knock,' he said, 'but you had the taps running. You can't have heard me. Anyway, why the sudden modesty?' Lisle was tugging the sweater over her head. 'There's nothing the matter with my memory.'

'And there was I thinking it was all a bad dream.' Lisle lifted her chin and stared at him. 'I presume you have something to say to me. Perhaps you'd say it and go.'

'So it's blunt speaking you're after,' he said reflectively. 'Very well. Lay off Oliver Grayson. He isn't fair game.'

Colour burned in her face. 'I don't know what you're talking about.'

He sighed. 'You had lunch with him today–remember?'

'Oliver happens to be an old friend,' she said stiffly.

'Lucky Oliver,' he said jeeringly. 'No wonder he couldn't keep his hands off you. But it won't do, Lisle.

He's a decent guy with one bad marriage already behind him. You're not going to screw his life up the second time around.'

'I've no intention of doing so.' She was shaking with temper.

'Well, you made a good start today,' he said derisively. 'Our subsequent meeting was a shambles. He wasn't thinking straight at all, and one didn't need to be Mastermind to guess who'd tied the poor man in knots. That's one of your specific talents, beauty.'

'Please don't call me that,' she said freezingly.

'Why not? You are beautiful—when you aren't using that enticing little body like a weapon.'

'And how does Miss Leighton use hers? Like a free gift?' She stopped dead, horrified. Her colour deepened. 'I'm sorry,' she apologised tautly. 'That was—indefensible. You seem to bring out the worst in me.'

'There seems plenty of it to bring out,' he returned drily.

Lisle was silent for a moment, mortified. Then she said huskily, 'I think it's time you stopped interfering in my life.'

'Stopped?' His brows rose. 'I haven't even started yet. And if we're talking about interference, perhaps you'd keep your delicate nose out of Harlow Bannerman's affairs.'

'I do work there.' She glared at him.

'There are various schools of thought on that subject,' he said softly. 'But I didn't mean the alleged labours for which you are so generously salaried. I meant your extra mural activities in the past twenty-four hours. The phone call to your brother warning him to get his chestnuts out of the fire, for instance, not to mention your lunch with Grayson.'

A dull flush rose in her cheeks. 'I've told you. . . .'

'And I'm telling you,' he said flatly. 'You're wasting your wiles, beauty. Oliver Grayson is bought and paid for, and it would take a damned sight more than having you in his bed for him to transfer his allegiance from myself to your brother. I presume that was the purpose of today's exercise?'

'Presume what the hell you like,' she said shortly, reflecting bitterly on the rotten luck which had brought them all together in the same restaurant. 'You think you have everything cut and dried, don't you, but being too sure of yourself can be dangerous. You surely don't imagine that Gerard is just going to sit back and see control of the company just vanish from his grasp?'

'This sisterly devotion is becoming absurd,' he said wearily. 'Gerard has never had control of Harlow Bannerman in his life, and nor will he ever have it. If it wasn't me, it would be someone else, but not your brother. He's wasted too many resources, upset too many people. The family name doesn't mean a great deal when there's no trust,' he added cynically.

She swallowed. 'So—what's going to happen to him, if you get your way?'

Jake shrugged. 'That's largely up to him, Lisle. He hasn't pulled his weight so far, and he's unlikely to change, no matter how big a fright he's had. He's had a number of warnings in the past, from your grandfather and others, and he's ignored all of them, so he can't hope for a great deal in the future. But I daresay he'll stay on in some capacity, somewhere where he can't do a great deal of damage.'

'I see.' Lisle was silent for a moment. 'And what's going to happen to me?'

He shrugged almost negligently. 'Nothing's been decided yet,' he countered.

'Really?' She sent him an amazed smile. 'Well, be sure and tell me as soon as it is. And now perhaps you'll get out of this house,' she added unevenly. 'Gerard will be back later tonight.'

'And you're afraid of a confrontation?' he asked mockingly. 'I had the impression that you loved them.'

'I don't have to explain to you,' she said. 'You're a

guest under this roof, Mr Allard, and an increasingly unwelcome one. Surely that's enough.'

'More than enough.' He stood up slowly. 'But don't you think Murray will wonder where I am—in the circumstances?'

'I'll think of some story that will satisfy him. After all, you're a very busy man. He wouldn't expect you to be dancing attendance here for ever.'

'Not on my future wife?' he enquired sardonically, and Lisle flushed angrily.

'Can we please forget that nonsense?' she requested tautly. 'It may amuse you. . . .'

'It doesn't particularly,' he said. 'And it may not be as instantly forgettable as you seem to think. Unless you want Murray to have a relapse by telling him it's all a sham.'

'Of course I don't,' she denied heatedly. 'But–oh, all this could have been so easily avoided. Why couldn't you have been honest with him when he first mentioned it—told him—well, told him there was Cindy Leighton?'

He looked faintly amused. 'I didn't think it was necessary. Knowing Murray, he's probably aware of her existence anyway, but why should he care? He may be straitlaced, but he's also a realist. And Cindy is no more interested in marriage than I am,' he added sardonically. 'In case that was worrying you.'

'I'm neither worried nor interested,' she said at once. 'Your—love affairs are no concern of mine.'

His smile widened. 'One of them nearly became your—intimate concern, last night,' he reminded her.

She looked back stonily. 'That is something else I'd like to forget.'

Jake laughed out loud. 'Well, that shouldn't be too difficult. There wasn't a great deal to remember.'

Not for you, she thought. Nor for you. For you—just another female body—another available girl. And if it didn't happen as you planned, then that's not

important either, because there'll be plenty of other
willing ladies to console you even after Cindy Leighton
has gone to the States.

Just for a moment, the knowledge caused her a pain
so sharp that she nearly cried out, then she was under
control again, except for a deep inner trembling that she
was unable to explain to herself. Or deny.

Someone else's voice seemed to say, 'That's true.
Well, goodbye, Mr Allard. It's been—educational, if
nothing else.'

'It has indeed,' he agreed. 'And it's not over, either.'

When he had gone, Lisle sat down on the floor,
staring in front of her, as if she'd been asleep, and woken
to find herself in a strange and hostile landscape. There
was a new and horrifying possibility clamouring for
attention in her mind and she did not want to hear what it
was telling her, or even acknowledge its existence.

Because it wasn't true. It couldn't be true.

She sank her teeth into her bottom lip, looking as if
mesmerised at the rumpled coverlet on the bed which
evidenced where Jake had been sitting, remembering
with hungry candour the lean graceful shape of his
body, and wondering with despair if she would ever be
able to look at him, or be in his presence again without
the memory of its naked warmth and strength against
her own, to torment her.

Murray was openly sulky when Lisle visited him alone
that evening.

'Where's Jake?' was his opening remark when she
entered his room, and it was clear that her carefully
worded phrases about 'Urgent business in London' and
being 'called away at the last moment' cut very little ice.

She held his hand. 'Aren't I good enough for you any
more?' she asked, teasing but a little troubled at the
same time.

'Of course,' he said a little testily. 'But damn it,
girl, I want you to get to know each other. There might

not be all that much time left, and I want to see you married before—before. . . .'

She lifted his hand to her cheek, her mouth trembling. 'Don't talk like that—please. You're going to be all right. You're much better. Anyone can see that.'

He looked at her as if he didn't see her. 'It should have been Gerard,' he said half to himself, 'but he isn't fit. I knew it, but wouldn't admit it. Far better if I had. But it's not too late. The Bannerman line will go on. Your children and Jake's—they'll carry the thing on, one day. That's the answer, and I have his word on it.'

Lisle heard him with dismay, wondering if she ought to press the buzzer for a nurse, but then he seemed to relax, and started to talk about something else in a normal tone, as if he had purged himself of his obsession at least for the time being, and the rest of her time with him passed without incident.

As she drove up to the house, she noticed there seemed to be lights on all over it, and as she entered the hall, she was aware of the loud chatter of the television in the drawing room.

Gerard was sprawled in one of the armchairs, glass in hand. He looked tired and bad-tempered.

'So there you are,' he greeted her fretfully. 'That was one hell of a flight!'

'When did you get in?' Lisle walked across and added another log to the fire.

He shrugged. 'A couple of hours ago—perhaps more.'

'It didn't occur to you to go straight to the hospital.' Lisle dusted off her hands and straightened, facing him.

'Frankly, no,' he said. 'I wanted a word with you first to find out how the land lies. You weren't the soul of clarity on the phone, you know.'

She said woodenly, 'Grandfather's had another coronary, but he's responding well to treatment. That's as much as I know.'

'Not that,' Gerard said irritably. 'Although naturally I'm relieved that the news is so good. What I need to know is what that damn Allard has been up to.'

Lisle gave him a level look. 'I hope that drink was strong, because you're going to need it.'

When she had finished her recital, he began to swear, a long, monotonous stream of obscenity which made her flinch. He hurled his glass against the mantelpiece, smashing the fragile tumbler into tiny fragments. Then he sat for a long time holding his head in his hands. When at last he looked at her, his face was as beautiful and as ravaged as a fallen angel's.

He said hoarsely, 'What the hell do I do?'

She knelt on the rug, collecting the broken glass into the palm of her hand with meticulous care. 'What can either of us do? We'll be lucky if we're both still working by this time next week.'

'That won't matter much to you, of course,' he said, and laughed suddenly. 'A marriage has been arranged—my word, how true! How very true. There's your new career, sweetie, just waiting for you to step into it. Mrs Jake Allard—the official title holder. There've been plenty of unofficial ones, but I don't suppose you'll mind that.'

She said with stiff lips, 'Not in the slightest, as there isn't going to be a marriage.'

'No?' He watched her smiling. 'I wouldn't be too sure—especially if Murray is recovering as well as you say. He's got something to live for now—his first grandson, out of Harlow Bannerman, by Allard International. He'll be able to set up his own private stud book.'

The broken glass cut her. She said unsteadily, 'You're foul.'

'I'm a realist,' he said. 'I'd give a year's salary plus expenses to be a fly on the wall during your wedding night. I don't suppose the groom's ever had a virgin before. I'll tell you something—you won't freeze him off like you've done all the others.'

Lisle felt sick. 'Gerard—for Pete's sake! We're on the same side—remember?'

'I'm sorry.' He slid to his knees beside her, sliding an arm round her shoulders in a protective gesture from their childhood. 'Really, I'm sorry. I don't mean it, you know that. It's just. . . .' His voice died away, and suddenly she saw how he would look when he was old. He revived almost at once, giving her one of his charming, coaxing grins. 'Cheer up, baby sister. We won't let it happen. I'll forbid the banns.'

A sound between a laugh and a sob caught in her throat. 'And Grandfather? I presume you'll go and see him tomorrow. You—you won't forget how ill he is. . . .'

'I won't forget,' he promised.

In the morning, she let him use her car to go to the hospital. She hadn't slept, and she didn't suppose he had either, but he managed a wry grin and a wave as he drove off.

As Lisle went back into the house, the phone began to ring.

She lifted the receiver and said, 'Hello,' and Janie's voice said, 'You're a dark horse, or is it an April Fool's trick six months too soon?'

'You tell me,' Lisle suggested.

There was an uncertain pause, then Janie said, 'You have seen the morning papers.'

'Not yet.' Lisle gave a small sigh. 'Gerard only got back last night, and we sat up until all hours talking, talking, and not really getting anywhere. We've only just finished breakfast, and he's gone to see Murray. Anyway, what's this about the papers?'

'It seems felicitations are in order—if that's the word I'm looking for.'

Lisle felt herself go very still. 'Janie, if you've something to tell me, I wish you'd just say it.'

'All right,' Janie said amiably. 'Congratulations, and can I be bridesmaid? That is if you're the Lisle

Bannerman whose engagement has just been announced to James Christopher Allard.'

There was a long pause, then Lisle said hoarsely, 'I don't believe it!'

'You're not saying it really is a hoax?' Janie whistled. 'Heads will roll for this! It's in all the leading dailies.'

'But it can't be,' Lisle whispered. 'It's just not possible. It—it was supposed to be a secret.'

'Then it is true!' Janie gave a little whoop. 'Wait till the gossip columnists latch on to it! From loathing to true love in twenty-four hours. How in the world did you manage it?'

Lisle said unsteadily, 'I'm not really sure myself. Janie, you're not fooling, are you?' This announcement is really in the papers?'

'Cross my heart and hope to die,' Janie assured her promptly. 'Lisle, what is this? You've hooked Jake Allard—he's wealthy, successful and incredibly sexy, and instead of girlish glee you're behaving as if you've been poleaxed. What's wrong?'

'Nothing,' said Lisle. 'Everything's fine. Look, Janie, can I ring you back later? I'm under rather a lot of pressure at the moment, and. . . .'

'Of course, love.' Janie sounded sympathetic. 'But I think you'll have to resign yourself that it's going to get worse before it gets better.'

Lisle replaced her receiver shakily. She could hear the front door bell pealing, the murmur of voices. When the library door opened, she turned, her face white and accusing, expecting it to be Jake.

But it was Mrs Peterson. 'Miss Lisle, some people have arrived. They've got cameras, and they say they want to interview you. Will you see them?' Her face puckered anxiously. 'You—you haven't had bad news, I hope?'

Lisle shook her head, trying for a reassuring smile. 'It's all right, Petey. It's nothing about my grandfather.

And I'd rather not see them. Will you send them away, please.'

Mrs Peterson looked doubtful. 'Well, I'll try, but I don't know—I don't know at all.' She went off, shaking her head.

As the morning wore on, Lisle began to feel as if she was under siege. The journalists didn't leave, but sat in their cars in the drive, waiting for her to appear.

'Fame at last, sweetie,' Gerard said acidly when he came back from the hospital. 'They're all out there trying to think of snappy headlines about romantic mergers.' He tossed a copy of one of the papers towards her, folded to the appropriate column. 'This is Murray's doing, you realise. He's like a dog with two tails this morning, trying to bribe the nurses to swap his water jug for a bottle of champagne. And where's the blushing bridegroom—maintaining a low profile? I can't say I blame him. One of the tabloids has got off the mark before anyone else with interviews with Cindy Leighton, and a couple of his other ex-ladies. You'll be pleased to hear that they wish you luck—they probably think you'll need it.'

Lisle's eyes were blazing. 'How could Murray?'

'Quite easily.' Gerard threw himself into a chair. 'Is that coffee? You might pour me some. I need a stimulant. Murray's delight in his own scheming didn't stop him putting me through the mincer. I thought he was supposed to be ill.' He accepted the cup she handed him, giving her a swift shrewd look. 'Look, love, I think you've gravely underestimated Murray's determination in all this. It may have begun as a sham as far as you're concerned, but it could end up being for real.'

Lisle said in a stifled voice, 'No, it can't—I couldn't. . . .' She stopped abruptly.

Gerard watched her frowningly. 'You know,' he said, 'if I didn't know differently, I'd say you fancied him.'

Colour burned swiftly in her face. 'You're being ridiculous!'

'I wonder,' Gerard said softly. 'I'm beginning to think perhaps you should go through with it.'

'But then you're not directly involved.' Lisle poured herself some more coffee with an unsteady hand, spilling some of it into her saucer. 'And Mr Allard has no more wish to be married than I have.'

'No?' Gerard raised his brows. 'Then I'm wondering why he let that notice go in. After all, he didn't have to submit to any more pressure from Murray. He could probably have talked him out of it, yet he didn't.'

She said curtly, 'I think he cares about Murray—actively wants his well-being, so why shouldn't he agree? Engagements can be broken, after all.'

'So can marriages.'

'Not as easily.' Lisle shook her head. 'But I don't understand the basis for this discussion. You don't want to see me married to Jake Allard, surely?'

Gerard sat silently for a few moments looking broodingly in front of him. Then he said, 'No, he's probably the last man on earth I'd choose as a brother-in-law in normal circumstances. But the circumstances aren't normal any more. Grandfather was quite brutally frank just now, and my life in the company—if, in fact, I have one—is going to be very different from now on.' He looked directly at her. 'Jake Allard's in the driving seat, and I have to accept that at least for the time being. If he has to be the chief, and I've got to work under him in some menial capacity'—his mouth curled—'then perhaps it might be useful to be related to him through marriage. After all, he's hardly likely to cause his new wife grief by throwing her only brother naked into the cold, hard world.'

'I wouldn't count on it,' Lisle said bitingly. 'It's a pity they don't award masters' degrees in self-interest, Gerard. You'd qualify top of the list.'

He spread his hand deprecatingly. 'I'm thinking of your interests as well, baby sister. What's going to happen to you in the big shake-up? Have you thought of that? You're not exactly qualified for very much, and even if you were, there could be problems when your engagement to Allard is broken off, however much of a fake it is. Whoever does the jilting, the other one is going to look foolish, and that's going to cause problems in the company.'

She drank some of her coffee. 'Of course, there is another solution. I could always marry someone else.'

Gerard gave her an admiring glance. 'I should go away more often! I left you a confirmed spinster. I arrive back, and you have prospective husbands coming out of the woodwork. Who's the lucky man?'

She hesitated. 'There's Oliver. . . .'

'Grayson?' Gerard gave a crack of laughter. 'That wimp!'

'He is nothing of the sort,' Lisle came back at him heatedly. 'I—I didn't mention it before, but I had lunch with him yesterday and—well,' she shrugged, 'there's a possibility. . . .'

'Oh, he fancies you all right,' Gerard said, grinning. 'His regard for you has always been in an inverse ratio for his loathing for me. But after today's announcement, our Oliver will be quite content to worship you from afar. He'll be working for Allard from next week, and stealing his woman will not be on the agenda.'

'I am not Jake Allard's woman!' Lisle almost spat. She was trembling again.

'As far as Grayson is concerned, you are,' Gerard said derisively. 'Suggest that he upsets his boss's applecart, and watch him run. He's a company man down to his silk socks, that's why he's always been so valuable. And I reckon him as a brother-in-law even less than I do Allard himself.'

'That's something I shall bear in mind, of course,' Lisle said scornfully. 'Shall I draw up a list of suitable names, and submit it to you for approval?' She stood up furiously, pushing back her chair. 'I'm going to ring Allard, and tell him to have that engagement notice

withdrawn—cancelled—whatever has to be done, and I
don't care how foolish we look.'

'He'll care,' Gerard commented. 'And so will Murray.'

Some of the fire was dowsed in her. She said, 'I was
forgetting.'

'But ring him by all means,' he said. 'I expect he has
reporters camped on his doorstep too, and it might be
interesting to know what he's telling them. You could
agree a joint statement, perhaps.' He gave her a small
bland smile. 'Unless you'd rather wait until tomorrow's
edition to discover the date of the wedding.'

'He wouldn't dare,' said Lisle between gritted teeth.

Getting through to Allard International was not
difficult. She asked for Jake Allard's office, and when
she gave her name on request, the girl on the
switchboard became almost frighteningly deferential.
She was put through straight away.

'Mr Allard's secretary,' said a voice.

Lisle bit her lip. 'Is Mr Allard there, please? This is
Lisle Bannerman.'

'Oh, Miss Bannerman.' There was real pleasure in the
woman's voice. 'I'm Mrs Pearce. I was so delighted
when Mr Allard authorised me to issue the notice of
your engagement. May I offer you every good wish?'

'Thank you,' Lisle returned, feeling awkward. 'If I
might speak to him, please.'

'Oh dear,' Mrs Pearce said, 'I'm afraid he isn't here.
He warned us last night that he would be away again all
day. Have you tried the flat?'

'Er—no.' Lisle thought bitterly that she hadn't even
known there was a flat. 'I suppose the number's ex-
directory,' she hazarded.

'Yes, of course.' Mrs Pearce sounded a little puzzled.
'But naturally you know. . . .'

'Oh, yes,' Lisle cut in quickly. 'It's written down
somewhere, but——' she managed a little laugh,
'everything's in such a whirl, I can't find it. Perhaps
you'd refresh my memory.'

'Certainly I will,' Mrs Pearce assured her warmly. She dictated the number, and Lisle wrote it down. 'And I want you to know, Miss Bannerman, that if there's anything—anything at all that I can do, you have only to ask. We're all very much looking forward to meeting you here.' She lowered her voice conspiratorially. 'Mr Allard is planning a little reception in your honour, you know.'

'Yes,' said Lisle, ultra-calmly. 'Mr Allard is full of fantastic surprises. Thank you for being so kind.'

She sat for a while staring at the numbers on the sheet of paper in front of her until they blurred and danced. She tried to formulate her thoughts, decide what she would say to him. Somehow she had to obtain the assurances she needed that it was all part of an elaborate sham, and that she was not being forced into a situation from which it might be impossible to retreat.

Slowly and reluctantly, she dialled the number, and listened to it ringing out, her heart thudding ludicrously as she waited for him to lift the receiver and speak.

It seemed to ring for ever, but at last she heard the click she was waiting for, and she tensed, moistening suddenly dry lips with the tip of her tongue.

Cindy Leighton's voice said huskily, 'Hullo—who is that?' Then, more sharply, 'Who's calling, please?'

Lisle put the receiver back on its rest very gently. The pain was back tearing at her, making her want to moan aloud. She knew what it was. She had known from the beginning, even though it was an alien emotion to her. She was bitterly, passionately jealous, and the reverse side of that wretched coin, unwanted and unacknowledged, was love.

CHAPTER FIVE

SHE had plenty of time to think. Since the start of the world, there had never been a longer day. The reporters tried a couple more times to persuade her to go out and talk to them, and pose for photographs, and eventually went away, thwarted and grumbling. Lisle was almost sorry to see them go, because at least their presence gave her a reason—an excuse to be uptight.

Gerard had given her an enquiring look when she came back from the library, and she had said merely, 'He's out of the office', thankful when he didn't press her further.

Later Gerard himself went out, to pay his respects to the village local and its hand-pumps, but she refused his invitation to accompany him.

Alone, she sat, trying to come to terms with what had happened, although she could still scarcely believe it. Could it be like that—could your whole life change irrevocably in just a matter of hours? She had always expected to learn to love, to be aware of its slow growth out of liking over a period of time. No one had ever warned her that it could flower inside her with such swift and overwhelming passion. Yet from the first moment, she had been conscious of that stark, unwilling attraction towards Jake. It had disturbed and harassed her, forcing her to behave out of character a dozen times and more. The fight had been on from the start, but her adversary had been herself.

Lisle groaned aloud. What an appalling, shattering mess she was in—in love with a man who openly despised her, even though her body had roused a transient desire in him, and involved with him in this farce of a fake relationship.

80

It was as if fate had suddenly turned on her with sharp teeth and claws to tear and rend her.

Gerard phoned later to say that he had met an old friend in the pub, and was going to play squash, 'to sweat out the jet-lag,' as he put it.

Lisle pulled on a jerkin and went for a walk through the fields. The house, which had always been such a sanctuary, seemed suddenly a box, its walls closing in on her. She could breathe better out in the air, but the slightly dank mist which was rising did little to raise her spirits.

She walked mechanically, almost unaware of her surroundings, her mind running on wheels round a well-worn and painful track.

If Murray lived, there would be increasing pressure from him to bring about a marriage between Jake and herself, and although Jake would eventually find some way out for them both, it was going to be an agonisingly difficult and embarrassing process.

If Murray died, and that was something she had to face too, then the problem of the engagement would be solved immediately.

But whatever happened, there would be heartache for her.

She had had to escape from the house because it held too many painful memories already. She had sat in the drawing room, twisting with pain as she remembered being there with him, his kisses warm and seductive on her body, trying not to think of him with Cindy Leighton in the familiar privacy of the flat she should have guessed they shared.

She should have realised too that they would be together. If Cindy was departing for the States soon, then it was obvious that she and Jake would snatch every opportunity to be with each other. She wondered if Cindy knew the truth about the supposed 'engagement', and remembering the expression in her eyes when they'd met the previous day, and the tabloid interview which Gerard had mentioned, thought it was probable that she did.

Perhaps they had even laughed about it together, secure in a relationship which did not need the convention of marriage, allowing them to enjoy each other without commitment. For a girl with a bright new career awaiting her, and a man who admitted openly that he was not interested in marriage, it was an ideal arrangement.

But not for me, Lisle thought wretchedly. I couldn't accept that kind of relationship.

But if that was all there was, whispered an inward voice slyly, you'd take it, then, and be thankful. Half a loaf has always been better than no bread at all.

Yet how would she have felt, she asked herself miserably, if she had given herself to him the other night, only to watch him go back to his mistress the following day? That would have been a hideous situation, leaving her pride, her self-respect in ruins.

To be taken, and then see him walk away, would be unbearable. But what would it be like, during this ghastly sham of an engagement, to be with him, yet always on guard against the betrayal of her deepest feelings? They couldn't always be metres apart. They were supposed to be promised in marriage, and people would expect them to seek each other out, to touch, even to kiss.

She stood still in the middle of the field, looked up at the lowering sky already greying into evening and said savagely, 'Oh hell!'

She trudged to the nearest gate and let herself out on to the lane. It was time she was getting back. Gerard would be wondering where she was, and if they were late at the hospital, Murray would be worried.

When she heard the car's engine behind her, she simply stepped on to the verge and walked on without even lifting her head, until she realised suddenly that its lines were familiar, and that it was slowing and stopping.

There was nowhere to run to, nowhere she could hide. In the pockets of her jerkin, her fists clenched convulsively, then relaxed.

Jake got out and stood beside the car, stripping off his driving gloves, waiting for her to come up to him.

Lisle felt as if her high russet boots were weighted with lead. She stood and looked at him gravely, her chin high, the green eyes questioning.

'Walking home?' Jake asked. 'I'll give you a lift.'

'I'd rather walk,' she said quietly.

His face hardened instantly. 'And I'd rather you drove—with me. Get in.' He opened the passenger door.

Wearily she sank on to the seat and waited tensely for him to join her.

He said, 'Didn't you notice it had started to rain?'

'Rain doesn't bother me that much.' It was true, but in the warmth of the car, her jerkin suddenly felt damp and clammy, and she shivered slightly. Jake sighed and reached into the back of the car, dragging forward a black leather coat which had been lying across the seat.

'Here,' he said brusquely, 'put this round you.'

'I'm quite all right. . . .' she began.

'Take it—or are you afraid of contamination?' She heard the sneer in his voice, and her lips tightened. She draped the coat round her shoulders, and sat looking rigidly ahead.

He commented, 'You seem surprised to see me.'

'I am. I thought I asked you to go.'

'You didn't ask anything, beauty, you told me, and that's an entirely different matter.' He started the car and it moved forward. 'I came principally to see what you wanted.'

'What I wanted?' she stared at him.

'Why, yes. Brenda Pearce told me you'd rung the office today, and I presume the anonymous call to the flat later was also made by you. You should have held on,' he added sardonically, 'I was only in the shower.'

Lisle bit her lip, hating the intimate picture his words conjured up. 'There was really no need to make a special trip,' she said. 'I only wanted to ask—why you'd announced our—our engagement, without even consulting me.'

'I did it because Murray insisted,' he said. 'I think he suspects our hearts aren't really in this manufactured courtship. As for consulting you, there seemed little point when I already knew what you'd say. I take it that I was right,' he added, after a pause. 'You weren't ringing to congratulate me on my initiative?'

'No, I wasn't,' Lisle snapped. 'Do you realise we've had a stack of journalists on the doorstep all morning?'

He looked amused. 'I thought you might. What did you tell them?'

'No comment.'

He laughed. 'You learn fast, beauty.'

'Not through choice.' That damned coat seemed to enfold her as closely as his arms, and she had to fight an impulse to tear it off and fling it through the window.

'Your mood is a little sour, darling,' he said mockingly. 'I shall have to think of something to make you feel more bridal.'

Lisle turned her head away in case one of those swift, searching glances discovered something in her face she would prefer to remain hidden.

At last she said, 'You surely didn't drive all this way just to say that.'

'No, I didn't.' He was braking smoothly, bringing the car to rest at the side of the road, and Lisle stiffened instinctively.

Jake sighed. 'There's a most unflattering look of panic on your face, Miss Bannerman. Relax—I gave up making love in cars in my salad days.'

'I'm not interested in your reminiscences,' Lisle said

tautly. 'Say what you came to say, and get back to—to London.'

Jake made an impatient, angry sound. He said wearily, 'All right, Lisle, we'll play this your way. Let me have your hand—the left one.'

She looked at him, her lips parted in bewilderment, and after a moment he reached across and pulled her hand towards him. The magnificent solitaire diamond flashed and glittered like a flame enclosed in ice as he slid it on to her finger.

'No!' Lisle said hoarsely, trying to tug herself free.

'Yes.' He did not release her. 'Murray expects it.'

'Of course,' she said bitterly. 'Just as Murray expected you to propose to me, just as he expected to see the notice in the papers. But what about me? Am I not supposed to have any feelings at all?' Her voice almost broke on a sob, then she added savagely, 'You will remember to call a halt to Murray's expectations eventually, I hope? Preferably before the honeymoon.'

'Well, we've established you don't care particularly for diamonds,' he said drily. 'But what have you got against honeymoons?'

Her shoulders sagged. 'In theory, nothing,' she said tiredly. 'I'm sure no marriage should be without one. It's just that I don't think I can take much more of this farce.' She looked at him, her green eyes wide and troubled. 'Please don't make me wear this ring.'

'You'd prefer emeralds? I'd wondered about that, myself. . . .'

'No,' she interrupted heatedly, 'I don't want any kind of a ring!'

He shrugged. 'It's just a convention,' he said. 'I didn't realise it might offend your liberated principles.'

He was misunderstanding her quite deliberately, she thought bitterly. She took a deep breath. 'It's a convention observed by couples who are genuinely engaged to each other. We are not. We are pretending to be engaged to fulfil some obligation you owe to my grandfather. I think this ring carries the pretence a stage too far.'

Jake gave her an ironic look. 'That was a nice little speech. Have you been rehearsing it?'

'Whether I have or not, I mean every word of it, and that's all that matters.'

'Not quite all,' he said. 'There's Murray. Like it or not, we've embarked on this sham together for his sake, and we're going on with it.' –

'For how long?'

'As long as it takes,' he assured her with grim emphasis. 'I'll take you to the hospital this evening, and when he sees the ring, he'll believe that I've started my wooing of you, and be satisfied. You can play your part by looking as if you've been swept off your feet just a little,' he added cynically.

Lisle looked down at the cold glitter on her hand. 'Naturally.' Her tone was dry. 'No doubt I slipped on the ice.'

He grinned. 'You're getting the idea, beauty,' he said approvingly, and the car moved forward again.

Gerard was coming down the stairs, as Lisle walked into the hall, Jake following closely behind her. She stopped when she saw him, and Jake paused too, putting a hand on her shoulder to steady himself.

Gerard smiled. 'Hello, young lovers,' he remarked. He looked at the ring, and his brows rose. 'Goodness, I didn't know they'd sold off the Koh-i-noor!'

Lisle gave a taut smile. 'Perhaps you'd get Jake a drink. I'll warn Petey that there's one extra for dinner.'

That accomplished, she went up to her room. For a long, long moment she stood in front of the full-length mirror studying herself minutely, then she went into the bathroom and ran herself a swift scented bath. The warm water relaxed her and took the chill from her tense limbs, and she towelled herself briskly until her body glowed. There was a favourite dress hanging in her wardrobe, stark black in a soft fine woollen material, long-sleeved, full-skirted, with a deep scooped neck. Against it, her skin looked like a pearl, and she left her throat deliberately bare, fastening the delicate diamond drops which had been Murray's gift to her on her twenty-first birthday into her ears. Her hair, brushed until it gleamed, she left loose on her shoulders.

The tension in the air was like a physical assault when she entered the drawing room, although on the surface everything looked calm, even amicable.

Gerard's smile looked as if it had been painted on as he greeted her. 'A glass of sherry, my sweet?'

She smiled her thanks and sank down gracefully on to the chesterfield, crossing her legs elegantly as she did so. She hadn't missed the sudden arrested expression on Jake's face as he'd turned to look at her, or the heated flare behind the grey eyes, and she felt an inward glow of satisfaction. He had told her to play her part, and she intended to.

'What have you been talking about?' she enquired lightly as she accepted her drink from Gerard.

Gerard grimaced. 'Harlow Bannerman—and my part in its downfall.' He attempted for equal lightness of tone, but Lisle could hear the note of resentment underlying it. 'This must be my day for hearing home truths,' he went on. 'Odd, my horoscope didn't mention it this morning.'

She saw Jake flash him an impatient glance, and groaned inwardly. Gerard so often picked the damnedest moments to be whimsical.

'How did the squash go?' she intervened hurriedly.

'Paul won easily, I'm afraid. He's become indecently fit since the last time we played, given up smoking entirely, and joined United Joggers or some ghastly thing. I'm to tell you, by the way, that you've broken his heart.'

She said wryly, 'I think it will soon mend.' She'd known Paul all her life, liked him, flirted with him and held him firmly at a distance. He was a born Lothario, with one broken marriage already behind him.

'You've had a telephone call too,' Gerard went on silkily. 'Oliver Grayson, and none too pleased either. But that might have been just because he found he was talking to me.'

Lisle gave him a dry look. 'Probably. Did he leave a message—ask me to call him back?'

'Not really.' A little smile played round the corners of Gerard's mouth. 'As I say, he seemed a little upset. He wanted to know if today's announcement was some kind of ghastly hoax, and then he rang off. I almost felt sorry for him,' he added cheerfully.

'Oh dear!' Lisle stared down into the amber depths of the sherry. She had caught a glimpse of Jake's face, the firm mouth set grimly, the grey eyes narrowed. A week ago, the news of her engagement to Jake would not have cost Oliver a single pang, although it would undoubtedly have surprised him. After her performance at lunch the previous day, he probably felt he was entitled to some kind of explanation.

She said, 'I'd better telephone him. . . .'

'I think not.' Jake's voice was quiet, but it held an inexorable note warning her that she defied him at her peril, that she had done enough damage already, and she felt herself flush.

Gerard was looking from Jake's rigid face to her mutinous expression with the light of unholy joy dancing in his eyes. 'Well, well,' he said softly. 'Not a rift in the lute already?' He gave Lisle a conspiratorial smile. 'Sorry, sweetie, perhaps I should have waited until we were on our own.'

Gerard, she thought in silent agony, for your own sake if not for mine, this is not the time for idle mischief-making. It was this predilection for planting barbs, she knew, which so infuriated Oliver Grayson and the other directors. She prayed Mrs Peterson would arrive to announce dinner, and thankfully heard the housekeeper's brisk footsteps approaching across the hall as if in answer to that silent petition.

She was about to leave the room in Gerard's wake when Jake's hand gripped her arm, detaining her. She winced at the bruising pressure of his fingers. 'What is it?' she asked.

'I meant what I said.' The dark face was menacing. 'You leave Grayson alone, you little tease! Things at Harlow Bannerman are going to be difficult enough without my second in command having fantasies that I've stolen the girl he loves.'

'He's not in love with me,' Lisle protested.

'But not for want of trying on your part, if what I saw at the restaurant was a fair sample,' he bit at her.

She tried to wrench herself free and failed, glaring up at him, her breasts rising and falling swiftly. 'What do you want me to say to him—that I wouldn't have him if he came gift-wrapped?'

'You don't have to say anything,' he said softly. 'I'll deal with him myself.'

'My goodness,' she jeered, 'anyone would think you were jealous, Mr Allard.'

'Anyone would be wrong, Miss Bannerman.' He released her almost contemptuously. 'I simply don't trust you, that's all.'

She walked ahead of him, her head held high, into the dining room. She supposed she had asked for that, but it had hurt just the same. As she helped herself to the smoked fish pâté, she noticed Gerard looking at her wrist, and realised there were angry red marks where Jake's fingers had gripped her flesh. Flushing, she pulled down her sleeve to hide them.

When the meal was over, Gerard excused himself from accompanying them to the hospital.

'In the interim period, Murray may have thought of some more of my shortcomings,' he said languidly. 'I'm sure the sight of two loving hearts in harmony will do him far more good.'

They drove to the hospital in silence. Through her lashes, Lisle watched Jake's cold, unyielding profile, weeping inside as she did so.

When he braked in the car park and switched off the ignition, she began to fumble for the door catch, but he said, 'Just a moment,' and she paused, turning her head to look fully at him, slight alarm widening her eyes.

'Before we go up to the ward, perhaps you'd tell me what it's all about,' he said.

'I don't understand.'

'Don't you? In our brief but momentous acquaintance I've seen you go from siren to schoolgirl, and now back to siren again. Why?'

She shrugged. 'You want me to play along. You can't complain if I choose to do so in my own way.'

'I wasn't thinking of complaining,' he said. 'So let's really enter into the spirit of the thing. . . .'

He pulled her into his arms, turning her so that she was lying helplessly across his body, and then began to kiss her, his mouth possessing hers in a ruthless and insatiable domination. For a moment she struggled, her hands beating frenziedly at his chest and shoulders, then as his lips forced hers apart, and the kiss deepened, she felt her senses drowning in sweetness, her resistance surrendering to the urgency of the moment.

She kissed him back, her response tuned passionately to his, her arms winding round his neck to draw him closer. His hand sought the soft roundness of her breast, his lean fingers, cupping, caressing until she moaned in her throat at the exquisite torment.

And then with shocking suddenness, she was free. Jake was pulling away from her, unlocking her arms from round him without gentleness.

He said harshly, 'That should add a little conviction to your performance.'

Almost before she knew what was happening, they were across the car park and approaching the main entrance. He was holding her arm, and Lisle had nearly to run in order to keep up with his long stride.

She said desperately, 'Jake—wait! I—I can't go in there looking like this.'

'You think Murray will be shocked?' he asked cynically. 'He won't. He'll be delighted. It will prove just how right we are for each other.'

Lisle caught a single horrifying glimpse of herself in the mirror in the foyer, her mouth swollen with passion, the lipstick blurred, her eyes enormous and fever-bright, spots of hectic colour along her cheekbones. No one was looking at her because they were all too preoccupied with their own business, but she felt all the same as if she was the cynosure of all eyes, and she was blushing all over as she stumbled beside him into the empty lift.

She said thickly, 'You think Murray will thank you for degrading me?'

'Is that how it was?' Jake asked cynically. 'Tell him I forced you, if it makes you feel better, beauty. Show him the bites and scratches and the bruises you made on me defending yourself.'

She shook. 'You bastard!' Tears were stinging at the back of her eyes, and aching in her throat. Convulsively, she forced them back, her nails digging into the palms of her hands.

She had more or less regained some measure of control by the time they reached Murray's room. He was watching the door eagerly, and a broad smile spread over his face when he saw them.

'You look wonderful!' Lisle bent to kiss him.

'So do you.' Even his voice sounded stronger, and the frail pinched look had vanished from round his nose and mouth. He lifted her hand, his eyes full of warmth and satisfaction, and studied her ring.

'A good choice,' he pronounced eventually. 'A diamond for my diamond of a girl.'

Lisle felt slow embarrassed colour steal into her face,

and she didn't dare even glance at Jake to see his reaction to this testimonial. She could imagine only too well the cynical amusement in his eyes.

'And where's that scapegrace grandson of mine?' Murray demanded.

'At home,' said Lisle, relieved that the spotlight was directed elsewhere. 'He's had enough bullying for one day.'

'Should have done it years ago,' her grandfather grumbled. 'Might have made something of him if I had. Perhaps it's not too late even now.' He sighed sharply. He directed another of his fierce glances at Lisle. 'Well, have you fixed the date of the wedding yet?'

She stared at him, confused and miserable, and lost for words.

Jake said, 'It's you we're waiting for—Lisle naturally wants you to be there, to give her away. We've planned a very quiet ceremony quite deliberately, so that it can be organised just as soon as you say the word.'

In many ways, it was the perfect answer. She recognised that, but his words chilled her blood because they made her realise that Murray might not get better and Jake knew it. She was very quiet for the remainder of the visit, which was occupied by a discussion of the way the following week's meetings at Harlow Bannerman would probably go. At any other time, she would have been fascinated, but as things were, she felt curiously detached from the whole thing as if it were no longer any concern of hers.

As they walked towards the lift, Jake glanced at her, brows raised. 'Why so silent? Outraged at my duplicity again?'

'No.' She shook her head. 'It—it was the right thing to say, and I know why you said it. It just isn't very easy to accept.'

'I can believe that.' His voice was dry.

As the lift descended, she said half to herself, 'But he looks so much better.'

'That doesn't always mean a great deal,' he said flatly. 'I thought you knew that.'

Lisle shivered. 'Yes, I suppose I did.'

She saw the grey eyes gentle to silver, saw him move, and knew that he was going to take her in his arms. She shrank in rejection. She was too vulnerable, and kindness from him at this juncture could well lead to total self-betrayal.

'Don't touch me,' she said hoarsely.

His hands were on her shoulders, their warmth burning her skin.

Lisle closed her eyes, swallowing weakly. 'I said—let me go. No one's going to be impressed if you maul me now,' she added savagely. 'Least of all me.'

His fingers tightened on her flesh so harshly that she almost cried out, then she was free.

More marks, she thought, fighting a little wave of hysteria. More bruises to hide. And deep within her heart, in the ungiven core of her being, a wound that might never heal, or would leave her scarred for life.

Silence closed heavily around them as he drove her back to the house. He had said over dinner that he would be returning to London that night, and she had expected he would leave right away. A drive through the evening, she thought, to the flat where Cindy Leighton would be waiting for him.

Yet he was right behind her as she walked into the house, where Mrs Peterson greeted them with the information that Gerard was out, and the offer of some refreshment.

'Some coffee, please.' Jake shed his car coat. 'Perhaps you'd bring it to the drawing room.'

Lisle hung back. 'I don't want coffee,' she protested. 'I'm going up to my room. I—I have a headache.'

Jake's mouth twisted contemptuously. 'You're being a little premature, beauty. Women usually save that excuse for after the wedding ceremony. Well, you can watch me drink coffee, if you really don't want any yourself, and we can talk. I think it's time we got a few things straight.'

'I've heard everything you have to say,' she said bitterly. 'Surely we don't have to go over the same ground again and again?'

'Well, you haven't heard this,' he said tersely. 'I think it's time this scheme of ours took a new direction, Lisle.'

'What do you mean?'

'I mean that we should abandon the pretence and do exactly as Murray wants. Get married.'

Dry-mouthed, she said, 'You're—crazy!'

'It's a crazy situation,' he acknowledged impatiently. 'We may not care for the way we've been thrown together, but Murray could have a point. I'm tired of service flats, and persuading company wives to act as my hostess when I entertain. It's time I married, had a place I can call home. And you're used to that kind of life. You could cope.'

'Yes.' She looked down at her hands, tightly clasped together in her lap, at the cold flare of the diamond ring. 'But women don't usually get married simply because they can—cope.'

'What is it that you want?' he asked. 'Financial security? A measure of sexual satisfaction? I think I can promise you those.'

Lisle bit her lip. 'It sounds so—cold-blooded.'

'It's an arrangement,' he said tautly. 'And who's to say that Murray might not be right, and that it might not work out well eventually.'

She gave him a direct look. 'But you don't really believe that?'

He shrugged. 'Let's say I'm willing to take a chance. How about you?'

She swallowed. 'I can't—I'm sorry.'

Jake stared at her for a long moment, his expression unreadable. At last he said, 'Let's leave it open, shall we? Give you time to think.' He hesitated. 'I have things to do this weekend, so I shan't be down. I presume you'll come to the office on Monday,' he added on a dry note.

She looked at him indignantly. 'Yes, of course.'

'In the past there's been no "of course" about it,' he said unanswerably. 'Perhaps you're proposing to become a reformed character as well as your brother.'

Her glance fell away. 'Your coffee's coming,' she said quietly. 'Perhaps you'd excuse me.'

The headache was genuine now, an iron band tightening round her temples.

Jake shrugged. 'If that's what you want.' He walked across to her as she rose to her feet, and put a hand under her chin, tilting her face towards him, the grey eyes cool and searching as they examined her.

She seemed to stop breathing, terrified that he was going to kiss her again, because if he did she would be lost, ready to promise him anything—even a loveless arrangement of a marriage.

But Mrs Peterson was already at the door with the tray, and Jake's hand fell away from her, enabling her to make her escape.

She found some aspirin in her bathroom cupboard and swallowed two. She sat on the edge of the bed, her fingers laced across her burning forehead as she waited for them to take effect, longing for the oblivion that sleep would bring, and knowing that nothing could assuage the pain inside her.

He had said he would give her time to think, and she knew what that would mean—minutes that would seem like hours, hours that would seem like days while she tormented herself with what might have been. What there could be still, she thought, as long as she didn't hope for too much, too soon.

He would not love her, but he had admitted that she could be useful to him and—faint colour stained her face—he wanted her. The urge to possess her ran strong in him still. Every time he touched her, she was aware of it, her physical sensitivity heightened by her emotional response to him.

It would be easy, she told herself yearningly, so easy to go with the tide, and accept the terms she had been offered.

Her mouth trembled suddenly, and she threw herself back across the bed with a little smothered groan. So easy, she thought, and at the same time—such a disaster.

CHAPTER SIX

THERE was a different atmosphere at Harlow Bannerman. Lisle noticed it as soon as she entered the building. It was as if some new and powerful dynamo had been switched on and was charging every corner of the company.

Lisle thought wryly that the source of that new power would not be far to seek. The place was buzzing with excitement on a more human level as well. When she went into the women's cloakroom, the high laughing babble of conversation between the assembled secretaries died as swiftly as if someone had snuffed a candle. There was an extra zing and sparkle about all of them this morning. It was evident they had all taken more than the usual trouble with their appearance, and half a dozen exotic scents vied for mastery over each other.

Now her arrival had reminded them that it was all a waste of time, Lisle thought as she intercepted one of the sidelong glances and interpreted the frank resentment it held.

Look, she had a crazy impulse to say, you think I'm a winner, the girl who has everything, but you're so wrong. I've had one hell of a weekend. I've hardly eaten, hardly slept, because every time I close my eyes I get this nightmare image of Jake with Cindy Leighton. She flew to the States this morning, you know, so this last weekend together must have been really special for them.

But of course, she didn't say any of that. She just went through the motions of taking off her coat and hanging it up, and pushing a comb through her wind-ruffled hair, and at last someone said in an embarrassed

97

voice that they were very sorry to hear about her
grandfather.

She gave her a cool, neutral smile and said, 'Thank
you. He's now making excellent progress.'

On the way to the PR department, she reflected that
that was no more than the truth. Murray was making
giant strides in his return to health. He had been moved
out of intensive care and into a private room on the
medical floor. He had clearly been disappointed by
Jake's absence during the weekend, but to Lisle's relief
he hadn't probed too closely for the reasons behind it—
but then he had too much else on his mind, she thought
ruefully.

He had talked weddings obsessively, balancing the
local church and a reception at the Priory afterwards
against a fashionable London ceremony and a hotel
wedding breakfast, with a dance to follow. Honeymoon
destinations he had brushed on too, and the initial
convenience of Jake living at the Priory while they
searched for a home of their own.

Lisle had let him talk, because he obviously derived
such deep contentment and comfort from it, and
she had answered him when he seemed to require
some response from her, saying the things she knew
he wanted to hear. And no one would ever know
what it had cost her, she thought with a little inward
grimace.

She went into the office she shared, steeling herself
against the inevitable thinly-veiled surprise at her
appearance. There were a few items in her in-tray, most
of them slightly yellowing round the edges in mute
evidence of how long they had been there, none of them
urgent or in the slightest bit interesting. It was the story
of her life, she thought, sitting down and examining a
fleck on her nail with minute interest.

The conversation between the others had wavered
when she entered, but it was gathering momentum
again now, although Lisle was prepared to bet there

had been an abrupt switch of the main topic. She felt sorry for her colleagues. Her presence in the office was invariably an inhibition. The usual complaints and grievances could not be aired in front of her because she was a Bannerman, and today they couldn't talk about Jake and the effect he might have on the company and their respective futures because of the diamond ring she wore on her finger.

Carl Forster, the head of the department, wasn't in his room. He was attending a meeting in the boardroom, along with the other executives. Lisle left the folder she had prepared on the Harlow Bannerman stand at the Salzburg Fair on his desk. She had worked hard on it, and there were some good ideas, but she knew they wouldn't be used. Jeff and Marian would have been working in the real promotion. Carl's suggestion that she should prepare a scheme had been one of the sops to justify her existence that he threw out every so often.

As she walked back towards her own room, she heard Marian's voice raised argumentatively 'Why should she care?' she was demanding. 'We all know she's only been filling in time before hooking some suitably wealthy guy. Well, she's managed that all right—and how. . . .' Her voice ceased instantly as Lisle pushed the door wide open and walked in. She saw Marian's flush of dismay and Jeff and Ian's obvious embarrassment, and walked over to her desk, not betraying by so much as a quiver that she had heard one word of what Marian had said, or applied it to herself.

Yet at the same time, it had confirmed something she had felt since she had arrived that morning—that something was deeply wrong. Her companions were usually civil, if nothing else, but today she had had the impression they were deliberately avoiding her glance.

She said, 'Does anyone know how the meeting in the boardroom is going?'

Ian smiled uneasily, 'Well, there's no blood actually running under the door.'

'But there must be rumours,' Lisle said lightly. 'There always are. The coffee must have gone in by now. Didn't anyone count the bodies?'

'There's going to be streamlining—rationalisation,' Marian said abruptly. 'That's what people are saying. That it's going to mean redundancies. This department hasn't been overloaded with work lately, and we're wondering which of us will be for the chop.'

'Last in, first out,' said Jeff with a little laugh. 'That makes it me, I suppose.'

Lisle stared down at the surface of her desk, her long sweep of lashes lowered to mask the compassion in her eyes. Jeff was hiding it well, but he'd only been married for a couple of months, and he must be worried sick at the prospect of unemployment.

Marian's outspoken remarks suddenly made total sense. There had been redundancies before, but they had mostly been achieved through natural wastage— people left for various reasons and were not replaced. Sometimes people even volunteered, usually because they wanted a change of direction and had another job planned.

As, Lisle supposed, it could be said that she had. That was what they would all think, naturally. If there was going to be a redundancy in the department, they would expect her to volunteer. And it was the last thing she had considered.

She had gone to Carl's room to tell him that she no longer wanted to be a passenger in the department, that she wanted to be part of the strength in real earnest. Jake's derision had achieved that, firing her with the wish to be more than the free-loader in the company that he thought her. She wanted him to see her as more than just a decorative body he would enjoy having in his bed, and facing him at the dinner table.

And she wanted too to have a career to immerse

herself in and stop her from thinking too hard about her emotional wretchedness. They reckoned hard work was the solution for many problems, and Lisle had come to work that day grimly determined on a fresh start which would reveal her as the hardest working member of staff in the company.

It would be cruelly ironic if she was to be robbed of her chance by sheer economics.

The morning passed with agonising slowness. A couple of times, she lifted her telephone and dialled Gerard's office, but each time his secretary's rather anxious voice informed her that he was still in the meeting.

It was lunchtime when Carl came down the corridor. He went straight into his room and shut the door while they all looked at each other with a kind of desperate surmise, then the buzzers on their desks began to sound, summoning them all.

He gave them a shadow of his usual buoyant smile. 'Sit down, everyone. What do you want first—the good news or the bad?' His eyebrows flickered upwards as he saw Lisle. 'Oh—Miss Bannerman. Mr Allard said you might be in today. He would like you to join him for lunch.'

They all waited politely for her to leave. She felt colour rising in her face.

'But if there's going to be a departmental meeting. . . .'

Carl sighed. 'Mr Allard is waiting,' he pointed out wearily. 'I told him I'd send you right along.'

To continue the argument would be undignified, but she felt totally humiliated just the same. The tacit decision that she was surplus to requirements had already been made, she thought, her cheeks flaming now with anger as well as selfconsciousness.

She said in a voice that shook slightly, 'Well, I'll leave you to your deliberations.'

She went out, closing the door behind her, although

she was tempted to slam it, but she didn't make her way submissively towards the managing director's office. Instead, she turned towards the Sales Department.

She said abruptly, 'Is my brother in?' to a saucer-eyed Miss Lawrence, and when the girl nodded, walked past her into Gerard's office.

His face was set with sullen resentment, but when he saw her he managed a travesty of his charming smile. 'How are the mighty fallen!'

Lisle seated herself on the edge of the desk, eyeing him gravely. 'What happened? All the rest of us have heard are rumours.'

'Well, rumour probably doesn't lie for once.' He was silent for a moment. 'Meet the new office boy. I'm out of Sales—permanently, as far as I can gather. No real responsibilities at all, or even lateral promotion.'

'In which department?' she asked sharply.

'His, of course. Presumably so he can keep an eye on me.' Gerard groaned. ' "Thou, God, seest me." I have a title of sorts, but assistant dogsbody is an accurate description if anyone's writing one.'

Lisle bit her lip. 'I'm sorry.'

'Save some of your sympathy for yourself,' he advised drily. 'His damned accountants have been going through the records, and they're less than impressed with the number of items that we've been allowed for expenses in the past. You're going to have to look for a cheaper flat, darling, and get your wine from a supermarket.' He sighed. 'And my Porsche has to go. It's not their idea of a company car at all.'

Lisle heard him almost with indifference. None of it would be any loss as far as she was concerned, she thought wearily. She had gone along with Gerard's suggestions and persuasions because he had insisted that they were all necessary, and that she was helping Harlow Bannerman, but she had never been totally convinced or happy about the role he had thrust upon her, and subsequent events had proved that all her reservations had been quite correct.

Gerard said savagely, 'And it couldn't have happened at a worse time. Carla will be back next week, and she does not go for losers.'

Lisle said gently, 'Does that really matter?'

'Yes.' He was silent for a moment. 'Hell, I was going to persuade her to divorce bloody Harry and throw in her lot with me permanently. I haven't a ghost of a chance of that now.'

She wondered if he ever had. The gorgeous Mrs Foxton knew exactly on which side her bread was buttered, and it was doubtful whether she would ever have been tempted to confuse the satisfaction of her sexual appetites with basic economics.

But at the same time it was disturbing to realise that Gerard thought of Carla Foxton as more than just another woman to add to his tally.

She said, 'Surely everything isn't lost? What about your seat on the board?'

'That's all right,' he said flatly. 'Not even Allard could take that away from me, although he probably wouldn't have bothered anyway. He knows I can't do much with all the rest of the men against me. They were all sitting there like the Three Wise Monkeys today. It was sickening.' He sent her a sidelong glance. 'The only amusing part was watching your boy-friend Grayson being slowly split in half. He clearly couldn't decide whether to be lost in admiration at Allard's methods, or as jealous as hell. Admiration may have won by a whisker this time, but I don't guarantee it will always happen.'

The door behind them was flung open and Jake walked in, the grey eyes raking Lisle mercilessly.

'I thought you might have taken refuge in here,' he said. 'Or didn't you get my message?'

'The royal command did get to me, yes.' She stood up. 'It didn't occur to you that I might not want to miss an important departmental meeting?'

'On your past record, frankly, no,' he drawled. 'Carl Forster seemed quite happy to release you, anyway.'

'He'd hardly be likely to argue with the new boss on his first day,' she snapped.

He gave her an ironic smile. 'I doubt if that aspect even occurred to him,' he said. 'Let's have lunch.'

Her shoulders sagged. 'I'm not very hungry,' she said tonelessly.

'And I don't have a great deal of time,' he said levelly. 'Shall we go?'

There were a number of restaurants in the immediate vicinity which Harlow Bannerman personnel used regularly, and she had assumed they would be going to one of these, but she was wrong. Jake went straight to the car park at the rear of the building, where his car was waiting. It was standing in the spot usually reserved for Murray, and seeing it gave her a pang.

'Where are we going?' she asked, as they turned into the stream of traffic.

'To my flat,' he said tersely. 'I want some peace and quiet, and a little privacy. It's been a hell of a morning, and it promises to be a devil of an afternoon, with half the company behaving as if I was God, and the other half as if I was Cesare Borgia.' He gave her a sidelong glance. 'And don't tell me which half you're in, because I can already guess.'

Lisle was rigid in her seat. 'I'd prefer to go back to the office.'

'Don't be a fool,' he said wearily. 'I've no time for a lunch-hour seduction, even if I was in the mood. We're going to the flat because it occurs to me that you haven't seen it, and perhaps you should.'

'I don't want to see it,' Lisle said immediately. 'It isn't of the slightest interest to me.'

'Then you're going to be extremely bored,' he said indifferently. 'Anyway, I thought looking round other people's homes was most women's idea of heaven.'

'I'm not most women,' Lisle shrugged. 'And I didn't think you looked on the flat as home.'

Jake shot her an amused glance. 'So you do hear some of the things I say to you. I'm surprised.'

The flat was situated in a discreet block, surrounded by private railed gardens, and the interior seemed to have been designed with the express intention of ensuring that the residents never bumped into each other. It was luxury personified, Lisle thought, looking round her, but impersonal luxury. . . .

The service was as efficient as anyone could have asked. Unseen hands had already laid lunch, not in the dining room, but at a small table by the huge drawing room window overlooking the garden. Cold chicken, Lisle saw, and a variety of delicious-looking salads, and a bottle of wine on ice.

Jake poured her a glass of pale dry sherry, then disappeared, taking his own drink with him, saying merely he would not be long. Slightly piqued and totally unable to relax, she sat gripping the glass and looking round her. It was a beautiful room, she thought, well-proportioned with a high ceiling.

Two massive sofas covered in cream velvet were stationed facing each other on either side of the fireplace, and all the occasional furniture had the patina and delicacy of the antique. There were few pictures or ornaments, as she had expected, but the alcoves which flanked the fireplace contained shelf after shelf of books, providing almost the only home touch, as far as she could see.

She looked at everything slowly and carefully, knowing in her heart that she was looking for traces of Cindy Leighton's presence and despising herself for doing it.

When the phone rang, she started nervously, nearly spilling her untouched sherry. She waited for Jake to answer the phone, telling herself he must be within earshot, but it continued to buzz at her angrily, and eventually she lifted the receiver herself, and gave the number.

'Hello, is that Miss Bannerman? I'm sorry to interrupt your lunch, but could I speak to Mr Allard? There's a tiny problem he should know about.'

The voice was friendly and familiar, and Lisle thought quickly. 'It's Mrs Pearce, isn't it? I—I'll try and find him.'

She went into the hall and looked round her doubtfully, wondering where he was. All the doors were closed except one, and she approached this hesitantly and peeped round it, speaking his name.

It was the bedroom, as she had guessed it might be, furnished in shades of beige and bitter chocolate, and starkly masculine. It was empty, but there were signs of his presence—the jacket he had been wearing tossed across the immaculate bedcover, and a discarded shirt on the floor. There was another door on the far side of the room, and beyond it Lisle could hear the sound of running water. She trod reluctantly across the thick beige carpet, and tapped on the door.

'Jake—telephone! It's your secretary.'

The noise of the water stopped abruptly, and seconds later he appeared, a towel draped hastily round his hips. He went straight to the extension telephone which stood on a low table beside the wide bed.

'Brenda? What the hell's the matter?'

He listened frowning, and Lisle told herself she should go back to the drawing room. She had given the message, and there was no reason for her to linger.

Yet linger she did, watching him obsessively, her eyes roaming over the broad shoulders, the deeply muscled chest, lean hips and long muscular legs. She was like a child outside a toyshop window, totally engrossed, utterly desirous of all she saw.

She swallowed deeply, trying to control the rush of her breathing, the uneven hurry of her pulsebeats, and saw too late that he was looking at her, that he had registered her absorption and interpreted it.

The silvery eyes narrowed, and he held out an imperative hand, silently ordering her to come to him.

As if mesmerised, Lisle obeyed. His arm went round her, drawing her against him, turning her into his body so that her mouth rested against the cool dampness of his skin. She was trembling as she began to kiss him softly at first then, as shyness dissolved in excited wonder, with passion, her lips tracing the strong hard lines of his shoulders in little feverish caresses, her hand curved like a benison over the deep urgent beat of his heart.

His fingers lifted the heavy fall of copper hair and cupped the nape of her neck, teasing her earlobe and the line of her throat with soft sensuousness.

As if in a dream, she heard him give swift, clipped instructions, heard the receiver go down on its rest, and tensed as his other hand rested on her shoulder gently, then slid down to her hip, pulling the lower part of her body into intimate contact with his. His head bent and his hard mouth parted the softness of hers in a deep, searchingly passionate act of possession.

The last remnants of sanity fled as she responded blindly and with her whole heart, clinging to him with unthinking ardour.

She felt the edge of the bed against her legs and it seemed natural and right that she should subside on to it, borne down into its softness by the weight of his body against hers.

Jake lay beside her, his hands framing her face gently, but his eyes looking into hers with frankly sensual urgency. He kissed her again, his mouth warm and erotically persuasive as it moved on hers, and a sigh of pleasure shuddered through her.

Her hands explored the length of his back, lingering on his spine, revelling in the silky glide of his skin under her fingertips, and she heard him groan softly against her lips.

He was undressing her without haste, his mouth
retracing the path of his fingers as he unfastened her
blouse, slipping the cream silk away from her body. The
tiny clip which fastened her bra was deftly snapped
open, and his lips brushed the fragile lace cups away
from her breasts before taking more intimate possession.
Lisle gasped helplessly at the warm, teasing provocation
of his tongue against her flesh, caught in the golden web
of pleasure and excitement that he was weaving so
effortlessly around her.

She felt him unhook the waistband of her skirt, was
aware of the slide of the zip, and she didn't care. All
that mattered was that this unhurried exploration of her
body with his hands and mouth should never cease.

The bed beneath her felt endlessly soft, like a cloud,
and she felt weightless too, drifting, the pressure of his
body against hers a beloved burden in her arms.

Languid with delight, she turned her head so that her
cheek brushed the quilted luxury of the bedcover, and
the scent of some alien fragrance wafted up at her. Not
Jake's. She knew the scent, the taste of his skin now, as
well as she knew her own. Not hers, either.

Her body stiffened in rejection as realisation dawned,
and she moaned hoarsely, 'No!', trying to twist away
from him across the width of the bed which he had
shared with Cindy Leighton.

Jake moved sharply, his arms, his body a prison
suddenly, holding her so that she couldn't escape.
'What is it?'

'Let go of me,' she said huskily, sick with self-disgust
because she had so simply, so readily forgotten.

'Why the hell should I?' he grated. His long fingers
gripped her chin, forcing her to face him again. 'You
started this, you little tease, and you're damned well
going to finish it!'

His mouth was hard now, and bruising, imposing an
aggressive mastery which she did not have the strength
to resist. His weight crushed her now, and she froze,

helplessly anticipating the brutal culmination, closing
her eyes to shut out the dark intentness of his face
poised above her.

A tear squeezed from under her eyelid and trickled
scaldingly down her cheek. Another followed it.
Another.

She heard him swear softly, obscenely, and then she
was free.

She turned on her side, her body hunched into a
curve of misery, and her hands went up to cover her wet
face. Silent sobs tore through her. She felt as if she was
breaking into small pieces. Cindy Leighton's perfume
seemed to fill her head, choking her, and she dragged
herself into a sitting position, pressing one clenched fist
against her mouth to dam back the small sounds of
despair.

Jake said harshly, 'Cover yourself, for Pete's sake.'

She heard him move away, back into the bathroom,
and then she ventured to open her eyes, snatching up
the scattered garments he had removed with such skill
and tenderness such a short time before and huddling
into them, her shaking fingers hardly able to cope with
the intricacies of buttons and hooks.

She scrambled off the bed and fled back to the
drawing room, grabbing her jacket, looking round
wildly for her bag, intent on flight.

Jake met her in the doorway, his arm implacably
blocking her passage.

He said coldly, 'Where do you think you're going?'

'Anywhere. Away from you,' she said, her voice
rising.

'It's a little late for that.' He was fastening a clean
shirt, slipping elegant gold links into the cuffs. 'We have
some talking to do.'

'I have nothing to say to you!'

'Then you can keep quiet and listen.' He gripped her
arm, propelling her inexorably back into the room,
thrusting her down on to one of the sofas. 'And calm

down,' he added impatiently. 'The only appetite I have left is for food.'

Lisle bent her head. She mumbled, 'I'm sorry.'

'Are you?' His voice was sardonic. 'You know all the tricks, beauty, but you nearly miscalculated with that last one. For all you knew, tears might have turned me on, and then you'd really have had something to be sorry about, you cold-blooded little tease!'

The raw anger underlying his tone made her shudder. Roused her defensive hackles too.

'You behave as if I'd intended this to happen, as if I'd planned it!' Colour began to creep into her pale face as she glared at him. 'It wasn't my idea to come here. And is it your normal practice to take showers in the middle of the day? And why didn't you answer the phone yourself when you've got an extension?'

'When I have a day as heavy as this one,' he told her, 'a shower—a change of clothes is a refreshment.' The grey eyes slid over her insolently. 'And an hour in bed with a willing lady is a bonus. I keep the bell on the extension turned off usually, because I don't wish to be disturbed in that part of the flat. Satisfied?' He waited for a moment, but Lisle remained silent. 'Now, have some lunch unless eating is something else you don't want to do with me.'

'I said I wasn't hungry,' she snapped.

'You did, didn't you.' His mouth slanted mockingly. 'Perhaps I should have taken your word for it, then I might have been spared this present ache in my guts.'

He went to the table, filled a plate with food, poured wine into a glass. Then he came back and sat on the sofa opposite.

The silence seemed to last for ever. Eventually Jake said, 'When you came into my arms just now, it occurred to me that it might be a tacit way of telling me you'd reconsidered my offer of marriage. Was I right?'

Lisle looked down at the thick pile of the carpet, and wished she was lying on it, dead. A dozen replies rioted in her head from flat denial to helpless submission, but she seemed incapable of uttering any of them. She knew what she ought to say, but she knew what she wanted to say.

Jake said inexorably, 'I'm waiting.'

She moistened her dry lips with the tip of her tongue, giving him a swift imploring glance. 'I—don't know. I need—more time.'

'Well, you're not getting it,' he said roughly. 'You're giving me an answer, one way or another, before you leave here today.'

'You're rushing me,' she said in a stifled voice.

'On the contrary, I'm practising superhuman restraint.' He finished the wine in his glass. 'I should have taken you to bed that first night. That would have settled all arguments.' He put the glass down. The grey eyes glinted at her. 'It isn't too late, of course. I could always phone Harlow Bannerman and tell them to cancel this afternoon's meetings because I have some important negotiations of my own to conclude.' He flung back his head and watched her, his face steely in challenge.

Alarm made her gabble. 'Isn't it a rather drastic way of gaining a hostess?' She tried to smile. 'With my record, aren't you afraid I'll ruin you with my extravagance?'

Jake gave her a sardonic look. 'No.'

'Not to mention my unreliability,' she went on with a kind of desperation.

'There are drawbacks to every relationship,' he said. 'At least we know ours in advance. And there'd be advantages too. You wouldn't find me—ungenerous, but of course I'd expect a fair return for my money. You won't be able to turn me off like a tap when we're married.'

'You bastard,' she whispered bitterly.

'My parents were married, actually,' he said. 'And, from what I recall, remarkably happily married too. No

doubt my mother will tell you some time. She lives in
the South of France these days because English winters
don't suit her, but she's flying into London next week
to meet you.'

'Oh, no!' Lisle lifted her hands to her face. It was all
going far too fast.

'Why not? We're officially engaged, darling—
remember? She might reasonably have expected to be
introduced to you at least before the announcement was
made.'

'It's all such a mess,' she said wretchedly. 'Oh dear,
I should never have let you talk me into this pretence. . . .'

'But you did, Lisle,' he said. 'So it's too late for
recriminations now. Too late for any more prevarication
too. Are you going to give me an answer, or do I come
over there and take it?'

She shuddered, closing her eyes, agonisingly aware of
the deep stir in her body. 'No—please! If you want me
to marry you, I will—on one condition.'

'I can't wait to hear what that is,' he said softly. 'A
plea to be spared the outrage of my vile and lecherous
attentions? If so, forget it. I want you, beauty, and I'm
going to have you wherever and whenever and however
I please. And don't pretend that isn't what you want
too, Lisle, because you aren't fooling anyone. Least of
all yourself.'

His words fell on her like hammer blows. She said
numbly, 'No, I suppose—not. But not here, Jake,
please. Please!' She opened her eyes and looked at him,
meeting the question in his eyes. 'This flat—I—I hate it.
I don't want to live here.'

He shrugged. 'Then we won't. I thought I'd already
made it clear that I wanted a proper home, and not a
pied-à-terre, but as a temporary measure. . . .'

'No, not even that,' she interrupted violently, her
voice shaking. 'And—and you can get rid of that bed
too!'

There was a silence. Jake's eyes narrowed in comprehension.

'Well, well,' he said mockingly. 'Afraid of ghosts, Lisle? There's no need.'

'Whether or not,' she said unevenly, 'that's the condition.'

A brief pause, then he said, amusement still quivering in his voice, 'Agreed.' He got up and came over to her, pulling her to her feet. His mouth took hers in a brief, hard kiss.

Like a seal on an agreement, she thought. Or a brand. Oh God, what have I done?

The questions haunted her through the rest of the day, even though she had plenty of other things to occupy her mind as well.

There was an air of gloom over the department when she arrived back that could have been cut with a knife. In the doorway she passed Jeff looking like death.

'What's happened?' Lisle asked as she sat down at her desk.

Marian's lip curled. 'Exactly what we predicted. One immediate redundancy, and a review in three months.'

'Who is it to be?' Lisle opened a drawer and extracted a tissue from the box she kept there.

Marian shrugged. 'We'll know later this week.' She sighed. 'Jeff's in a hell of a state. He and Cathy had just moved into a new house.'

She sighed again and began to type rapidly. Lisle sat staring down at the top of her desk, examining the grain in the wood as if it had some hypnotic quality. Eventually she reached for the memo pad and wrote out her resignation, and took it in to Carl, who accepted it without surprise, and even, she thought, with a certain relief.

She cleared her desk, aware that the others were watching her covertly, but offering no explanations as

she sorted out and discarded. There was nothing left for
her here, she had chosen an alternative path in life, so
she might as well leave.

She was conscious too of a subtle shift in attitude.
When Marian went to the machine for coffee, she
brought Lisle one too.

And later Jeff said awkwardly, 'Carl was showing us
some of the ideas you had for the Salzburg thing. They
were spot on.'

'Thanks,' she said lightly. 'All I ever wanted was to
be given a chance.'

When she stood up to go, they all shook hands and
wished her well, and she responded courteously.

As she walked along towards the stairs, she heard
someone call her name, and glancing round saw Oliver
Grayson standing in the doorway of his office.

She said with faint embarrassment, 'Hello, Oliver. I
thought you'd be tied up in this meeting all afternoon.'

He grimaced. 'We've been allowed a fifteen-minute
break, and boy, do we need it!' His eyes searched her
face. 'Lisle, what's going on? That notice in the paper—
is it genuine? I got the impression. . . .'

She flushed, knowing exactly what impression he had
been given. 'It's all true. Jake Allard and I are engaged.'
She bent her head. 'I can't explain. I don't really
understand it myself.'

'But you're clearly not happy,' he said in a low voice.
'Even a casual observer can see that, and I don't claim
to be that. You don't have to do it, Lisle, no matter
what the pressure. Let me help you.'

He had possessed himself of her hand, and she tried
to withdraw it from his grasp, her eyes full of
trouble.

'No one can help me,' she said tiredly. 'I've behaved
very badly, Oliver, and I don't know how to apologise.
Anything I can think of sounds inadequate.'

'You're being forced into this,' he asserted, his eyes
fixed on her intensely. 'I know there are problems,

Lisle, but you don't have to go to those lengths to solve them. Don't shut me out, my dear. It's not too late.'

Jake said very drily, 'It's getting later all the time, Grayson. The meeting's ready to start again, if you are.'

Lisle gasped. She hadn't heard him approach, and had no idea what he had heard or the interpretation he might place on it, but the grim expression in his eyes as they rested on her was hardly reassuring.

Oliver released her hand as if it had scorched him, and muttering something barely audible, turned away towards the boardroom.

'Just a moment.' Jake's hand gripped Lisle's shoulder. 'Where do you think you're going?'

'I no longer work here,' she said quietly. 'I resigned.'

'Very wise. While you're in the mood for giving notice, you can tell your flatmate that you're leaving too. Get your things packed, and I'll come round later and drive you down to the Priory.'

'But I can't,' she protested. 'Not just like that. It's unfair to Janie. . . .'

'I'll make sure she doesn't suffer financially,' he said. 'And there'll be no objection from the landlord either.'

'But I could stay at the flat until our notice expires. . . .'

'You could, but you won't.' There was ice in his voice. 'It's time your wings were clipped, beauty. I told you I wouldn't stand for any more games with Grayson, and I meant it. You're going down to the Priory tonight, and starting to learn how to behave yourself.'

'It wasn't as you thought,' she said in a low voice.

'No?' His tone was cynical. 'If you want me to believe that, you shouldn't allow him to fondle you in a public corridor.' His voice roughened. 'Whatever you've done in the past, Lisle, from now on I have exclusive rights in you, and I'm prepared to enforce them if I have to. I presume that's something you'd prefer to avoid?' He paused, taking in her pallor, the sudden rigidity of her feelings, and his fingers relaxed their grip, setting her free. 'Go and pack,' he directed quietly.

Lisle had an insane urge to fling herself into his arms, to tell him that neither Oliver or any other living man meant a thing to her, that she loved him and only him, and she would do anything, be anything he wanted if only—only he would love her in return.

But he was already turning and walking away towards the open door of the boardroom where people were already gathered awaiting his arrival, and the moment, if it had ever existed at all, was lost.

She watched the door close behind him, and then she went down the stairs, alone.

CHAPTER SEVEN

LISLE was already half packed by the time she heard Janie's key in the door. She went into the hall to meet her. 'Surprise!'

'Welcome home.' Janie's eyes ran over her critically. 'You look a little fraught, but that's hardly surprising under the circumstances.' She gave an ecstatic sniff. 'Food—you angel!'

'Only a casserole.' Lisle gave her a strained smile. 'It seemed the least I could do. And I only hope you still think I'm an angel when I tell you the news.'

She pushed open the bedroom door and let Janie see the cases lying open on the bed.

Janie's brows lifted. 'My word, the speed of light must seem like a crawl when Jake Allard's around! When's the wedding? Yesterday?'

'Almost', Lisle said ruefully.

'And why not?' Janie gave an approving nod. 'There's nothing to wait for, after all, now that ice of yours has finally cracked. I'm only thankful it's been for Jake Allard and not one of Gerard's so-called friends. That brother of yours must be on terms with every rat in London, and not all of them male,' she added.

There was something in her voice suddenly which made Lisle look at her curiously, her sensitivity heightened by her own emotional turmoil. But instinct told her that Janie was raw, and would not welcome questions, however caring or well meant.

They ate the meat and vegetable stew she had prepared in the kitchen, then, while Janie washed up and cleared away, Lisle went on with her packing. She would miss Janie badly, especially the shrewd caustic streak which her almost doll-like blonde prettiness concealed.

She was sorely tempted to confide in her, but something held her back. A feeling, perhaps, that no advice, however good, would help her to a solution, coupled with a conviction that Janie had problems of her own. She wondered rather bitterly how she could have been so blind and self-centred.

'Perhaps a change all round will be a good thing,' Janie said abruptly, as they had sat over their coffee. 'It's easy when you're comfortable to get into a rut, and I can't keep this place going on my own. I'll start looking for somewhere else—maybe join forces with Anita at the office. Her flatmate's getting married too.' She gave Lisle an uncertain grin. 'But we'll keep in touch.'

'Of course,' Lisle returned lightly. 'Chief bridesmaid, no less.'

She worked like an automaton, but she still wasn't ready when the doorbell rang.

She called, 'I'll get it,' to Janie, and opened the door. Jake was lounging on the doorstep. His eyes met hers with irony.

'Full circle,' he commented. 'Ready to go?'

'Not quite. I—I seem to have more things than I thought. Does it have to be this evening?' She sent him a pleading look. 'If I had another day. . . .'

'This evening,' he said implacably. He gave her a long, hard look. 'Perhaps I don't like ghosts either.'

Lisle flushed unhappily, turned away. What use were denials, when they would not be believed? she asked herself. Perhaps when she was his wife, and he had had indisputable proof of her innocence, he might think again.

'Then maybe you wouldn't mind waiting,' she said in a constricted tone. 'I'm sure Janie will give you some coffee.'

He nodded and turned in the direction of the kitchen.

Lisle flew round, cramming the last items into her cases. She was only packing clothes, but there were other things she simply didn't have space for, or time to collect—ornaments, and some books and records, and a few pictures she'd bought, inexpensive prints mostly, but she liked them, and didn't want to leave them. She'd come back, she thought, at some convenient time and gather them all up.

Janie came to the kitchen door and watched as Jake fetched Lisle's cases from the bedroom.

She said with an exaggerated sigh, 'I do like a masterful man.'

He grinned at her. 'We're a dying breed.'

She groaned. 'Does that mean you haven't a brother?'

'Not even a second cousin twice removed,' he told her regretfully.

Watching them, Lisle thought how much she would give to have Jake look at her with the same lazy admiration in his grey eyes, the same genuine warmth in his smile. Cindy Leighton had been blonde, she thought, probing the wound to find if it still hurt, and receiving a very painful affirmative, so perhaps blondes were Jake's preference.

She said a muted goodbye to Janie, promising to phone her as soon as she had any definite plans, and followed Jake down to the car.

As he took his place beside her, he sat wearily for a moment, staring at the dashboard.

Lisle moved impulsively, placing a hand on his arm. 'Drop me at the station. I can make my own way from there,' she urged. 'You've had a lousy day. You can't want to drive all those miles.'

'Perhaps not, but I intend to just the same.' His mouth twisted. 'And drop the cossetting note, Lisle. That isn't what I want from you at all.'

Her glance fell away. She said huskily, 'What *do* you want, Jake?'

'I thought I'd made it clear,' he said. 'I want your social acumen, and your body, not necessarily in that order. Is there anything else you want to know?'

'No,' she said, dry-mouthed. 'I think that just about covers it.'

She shrank down into her seat, as if she was composing herself for sleep, but behind her closed eyes and surface calm, her mind ran in circles like a small caged animal, looking in vain for escape.

Jake said nothing more to her and she was thankful in some ways for the respite, but at the same time she wondered if that was to be the pattern of their marriage—confrontation at both mental and physical levels, interspersed with long silences, and, if so, how she could bear it. It was in conflict with every small ideal she had ever had about the relationship between husband and wife.

When they arrived at the house, she looked at him uncertainly as he took her cases from the car, wondering if he intended to leave immediately. But the question was answered for her when Mrs Peterson came to welcome them with the information that she had prepared some sandwiches and would bring them to the drawing room with a tray of coffee as soon as they were ready.

'You did say that was all you wanted, Mr Allard,' she added, giving him a worried look. 'But it would take no time to cook you something, if you'd prefer.'

Jake smiled at her, the tired lines on his face relaxing. 'The sandwiches will be fine,' he said. 'Shall we say ten minutes.'

'Just as you say, sir. And I've made up the bed in the room you had before. I hope that's satisfactory.'

When they were alone, Lisle said tautly, 'I didn't realise you planned to stay the night.'

He lifted his brows. 'Any objections?'

'I suppose not.'

'Graciously spoken,' he jeered. 'What happened to

the womanly solicitude you were brimming with in London? I thought at the time that, if closely examined, it would turn into an overwhelming desire to be rid of me any price.'

Lisle shrugged. 'If that's what you want to think. . . .' she said colourlessly.

'Half the time, I'm damned if I know what to think,' Jake said, his tone curiously bitter, and she glanced at him quickly, wondering if he was beginning to have second thoughts about the cold-blooded arrangement to which he was condemning them both.

She said, 'I've already eaten. If you don't mind, I'll go up to my room. It's getting late and I want to unpack those cases before everything gets too crushed.'

His face was inscrutable. 'And if I do mind? You're going to be my wife. Perhaps I'll want you to help me relax, smooth away the knots. Isn't that what good wives are supposed to do?'

She was tied in knots herself. She looked across the room at him, her eyes widening in a kind of mute appeal.

Jake swore softly under his breath. 'Run along,' he said impatiently. 'You look as if you're about to collapse.'

She felt like it too. Her room seemed strangely alien as she moved slowly around it, putting things on hangers, making space for them in cupboards. It was strange to think that most of the nights of her childhood and girlhood had been spent inside these four walls, because they said nothing to her now. That child, that girl might never have existed.

She looked at herself distrustfully in the mirror. She looked the same, although a little pale and strained. How was it possible to look the same, and yet be so deeply, irrevocably changed, and how could it happen so quickly? She could count the time she had known him in days still, and yet it made no difference.

The girl who had dreamed her dreams in this room

was gone for ever, and Lisle knew that even if time could run backwards and the last week be wiped away, that would not be her choice.

Even on his own terms, she wanted Jake. For better or worse, she thought ironically.

The knock at the door wasn't particularly loud, but it seemed to reverberate through the room.

Mrs Peterson would never have knocked like that, Lisle thought, hugging the sweaters she was holding defensively against her breasts. She had undressed earlier. She was wearing her nightdress and robe, and she was tempted to take one flying leap into bed, sweaters and all, pulling the covers over her head and pretending to be asleep. Except that he wouldn't be fooled for a moment.

The knock was repeated impatiently, then the door opened and Jake walked in. His eyes raked her mercilessly.

'Turned deaf and dumb?' he asked sarcastically.

'No,' she said. 'I just didn't want to be disturbed. For all you knew, I could have been asleep.'

He shook his head. 'I've heard you pacing up and down, backwards and forwards. I knew you were awake.'

'But that doesn't mean I necessarily want company.'

'Oh, quit complaining,' he said wearily. 'If you imagine this stop-go policy of yours has filled me with insatiable lust, then you're wrong. I've had a swine of a day, and I'm in no mood for bedroom games, especially when they're of the inconclusive variety that you seem to favour. I prefer to wait until I have the legal right to enforce any demands I make on you. I hope that sets your mind at rest,' he added sardonically.

'Wonderfully,' said Lisle. 'I feel like the man who was told he'd been granted a stay of execution because they were building a bigger and better gallows. Perhaps now you'll tell me what you do want.'

'I just wanted to let you know that I'd rung the

hospital, and Murray has had a fair day. I apologised for our failure to visit him, but they seem to feel he'd already had too many visitors today as it was. I said that you'd be along tomorrow.'

She flushed dully, remorse striking at her. She'd been so tied up in her own emotions and confusions that she'd hardly given her grandfather a thought.

'Yes, of course,' she said constrictedly. 'Thank you for telephoning. I—I should have done so myself.'

Jake shrugged. 'Think nothing of it. I am genuinely fond of Murray, you know. It isn't just gratitude because he once gave me a helping hand.'

'Or the favours he's done you since,' some demon prompted her to say.

His brows lifted. 'Now what do you mean by that?' he challenged. 'If it's Harlow Bannerman, I'd hardly regard digging the company out of its self-inflicted mire as a particular privilege. Or were you thinking along more personal lines, beauty?'

'Don't call me that,' she protested heatedly.

'Why not? It's no more than the truth.' The grey eyes moved over in total reminiscence, making the blood flare in her face. ' "But beauty's self she is," ' he murmured. 'I'm sure you can supply the rest of the quotation.'

She could, only too well, and on a reflex action, her hands moved to tighten the already secure sash of her robe. Jake laughed, and she turned away, hotly embarrassed, at that little piece of self-betrayal.

'If you were referring to yourself,' he said drily, 'there've been damned few favours going so far. Not that I've been on my knees begging for them either, of course.'

'Of course,' Lisle agreed with a snap. 'But then no man in your income bracket ever has to beg—does he?'

'Not often,' he agreed, apparently unruffled by her waspish taunt. 'And I have no intention of starting either, so be warned, beauty. I take what I want.'

'And pay for it?' Her mouth curled.

'Whatever I consider it's worth.' He sent her a

mocking look. 'Take care you don't pitch your price too high, Lisle.'

'And if I do—what then?' she said. 'Will you—cancel the contract?'

'No way, beauty.' Jake's grey eyes glinted at her. 'Merely re-draft its terms in a way you won't like.'

'In the same way as you're re-drafting Harlow Bannerman?'

He smiled. 'Not quite.' His glance sharpened. 'I take it you disapprove of my methods?'

'It's no longer any of my business,' she said bitterly. 'I don't work there any more—remember?'

'But that won't stop Gerard crying on your shoulder,' he commented brusquely. 'When he does, you might bear in mind that he's brought his troubles on himself.'

'Then his—demotion is an additional punishment.'

'Demotion? I'd hardly call it that.' Jake's voice slowed to a drawl. 'He's going to learn how to tackle a job properly, instead of being allowed to play ducks and drakes with the Sales Department. Where's the hardship in that?'

'Oh. You make it all sound so terribly reasonable,' she said bitterly. 'But you know as well as I do that you're slapping him down.'

'Perhaps someone has to. Would you rather it were Harry Foxton—because that could be on the cards too.'

Her head came up with a jerk, and she stared at him, her eyes dilating. 'What do you mean?'

'Do I really have to spell it out? You can't make the running with a spectacular lady like Carla Foxton and expect the world not to notice. And, generally, when people have stopped looking, they start talking. Word soon spreads, and contrary to what they say, the husband isn't always the last one to find out.'

Lisle bit her lip, dismayed. 'What do you think will happen?' she asked eventually, in a small voice.

Jake shrugged. 'I'm not Harry Foxton. He should have made sure Carla's stable door was bolted from the day they were married instead of indulging in useless recriminations when it's too late. As it is—I know some of his cronies, and they reckon he's hitting the bottle hard and that when he does, he becomes mean.'

Lisle moistened her lips with the tip of her tongue. 'He—he really loves her—Gerard, I mean. He was going to ask her to leave her husband and be with him.'

'Can he afford her?' Jake asked cynically. 'By all accounts, she's another over-priced woman.'

'He can't now, certainly.'

Jake gave a crooked smile. 'If that's a subtle accusation that I've put a spoke in the wheel of true love, forget it. The present Mrs Foxton loves herself and Harry's money with almost equal degrees of passion, and I wouldn't think Gerard even features in the ratings, except incidentally.'

She couldn't accuse him of being unfair, because his summation of the situation coincided with her own.

'Do you speak through—bitter experience?' she asked at last.

He gave her a sardonic look. 'Let's say I know the type. As you were shrewd enough to point out, my income bracket has seen to that.' He paused. 'After all, beauty, you wouldn't be marrying me if I was poor.'

The jibe caught her like a whiplash, and Lisle stiffened, words of angry denial already forming on her lips until she realised, just in time, what their utterance would imply.

She had almost told Jake that she would want him no matter what the circumstances, even if he became a penniless bankrupt tomorrow. She had almost told him that she loved him, and wanted nothing more than to be his wife. And what a damaging, abject admission that would have been in the circumstances!

I want your social acumen and your body,' he had said, only a short while ago. Love wasn't a word he was prepared to include in the vocabulary of their relationship.

So she could not be the one to introduce it. At the very least, he would be embarrassed; at the worst, he might laugh. And she could not risk either reaction. It would cost too much of the tender, vulnerable emotion she nurtured so secretly.

'You're very quiet,' he mocked. 'Trying to think of a way to break it to me gently, Lisle?'

Her nails dug sharply into the palms of her hands, but the smile she sent him was light and taunting.

'Why should I? You know as well as I do, Jake, that I wouldn't be marrying *anyone* if he was poor.' She smothered a little yawn. 'And now perhaps you'd let me have my room to myself again. I'm a little tired.'

'How unfortunate,' he said too pleasantly. 'Because our little chat seems to have revived me completely. Perhaps I no longer want to leave you to your own devices for the remainder of the evening.'

Alarm was flaring along her nerve-endings, sending disquieting prickles down her spine. Her voice was steely. 'I'd be glad if you'd get out.'

'I'm sure you would. In fact, you'd probably be delighted if you could make me vanish completely with one snap of your fingers.' He took a step towards her. 'Only I'm not vanishing, Lisle. Not now. Not later.'

She recoiled, stumbling over the trailing hem of her robe, and sinking ignominiously to her knees on the pile of sweaters she'd let fall to the floor earlier.

Jake laughed. 'Now who's begging?'

'Leave me alone!' she shouted, as he reached down to pull her to her feet again. 'Don't you lay a finger on me!'

'I'm going to lay a damned sight more than that on you,' he grated, molten anger searing in his voice.

Lisle shuddered, shrinking away from him. 'Jake—please! You—you said you were going to wait—until we were married. You said so.'

'Then here's the first lesson of the evening—it isn't

only women who are allowed to change their minds.'
His hands slid inexorably beneath her arms, lifting her.

'No!' Her hands flailed wildly at his chest. 'I'll hate
you!'

'Tell me something new.' He bent his head, kissing
her savagely, grinding the softness of her mouth against
her teeth with unyielding passion. He dragged the
neckline of her robe apart, his hands seeking her
breasts, caressing the hardening peaks until she sobbed
aloud in passionate torment. He said hoarsely, 'But one
way or another, Lisle, I'll make you admit that you want
this as much as I do.'

It was true. It was true. How could she deny it when
her whole body was yielding faintingly against his? Yet
that one admission, if uttered, might bring others,
infinitely more damaging, tumbling from her trembling
lips.

He tossed her down on to the bed, and she lay there
looking up at him, dredging up from deep inside her
some of the old insolence and bravado, forcing a smile
to her mouth.

'This—yes.' She let her hands drift caressingly down
her body, watching his eyes darken sensually as she did
so. 'But not—you. Not particularly. Unfortunate, isn't
it?'

He was very still suddenly, incredulity warring with
anger in his unmasked expression.

He said quietly, 'Unfortunate for you, certainly, if
you think it makes the slightest difference to me or our
bargain then think again.'

Lisle allowed her eyes to widen contemptuously.
'You mean you don't care?'

'If I had any illusions about you, beauty, I might.'
His smile was thin-lipped. 'As it is. . . .' His glance
flicked her before he turned away. 'Sleep well, my bride-
to-be.'

She lay for a long time looking at the closed door,
feeling the ache deep in her body, and wishing with a

kind of futile weariness that the temporary oblivion of sleep would claim her.

It was late, and he was long gone by the time Lisle stumbled downstairs in the morning, Mrs Peterson exclaimed at her pallor and suggested a day's rest would do her good, but Lisle could imagine nothing worse than more silent hours spent in her bedroom, staring at the ceiling, trying to figure out a way to escape from the emotional maze she was trapped in.

She had half wondered if there might be a message waiting for her from Jake, at least to tell her when she could next expect to see him, but there was nothing, and she felt she couldn't ask the housekeeper if he had given any indication as to when he'd be visiting the Priory again. Mrs Peterson would think it distinctly odd for her to be so ignorant of her fiancé's plans.

She worked in the garden for a couple of hours. It was a dry misty day with all the threat of winter in the chilly breeze, but the fresh air and exercise helped revive her.

After lunch, she went to see Murray. She had expected him to question her over her decision to leave Harlow Bannerman, but to her surprise he seemed to regard it as a natural consequence of her engagement.

'There are a great many arrangements to be made, details to be worked out,' he said, frowning.

Lisle put her hand over his. 'Not that many. It's going to be a very quiet wedding. We—we both want it that way.'

He gave her a suspicious look. 'Why, for heaven's sake? Anyone would think you were ashamed! I'm not giving my only granddaughter away at some hole-and-corner affair.'

'And I'm not playing the leading role in a public performance, even if it is stage-managed by you,' she returned calmly.

For a moment his scowl deepened, and then he gave a bark of laughter. 'Well, have it your own way, I suppose.'

'What a concession!' she teased. 'While you're being so submissive, can I ask you to place an embargo on non-family visitors. Sister stopped me on the way in to complain. She said there was a never-ending stream of people in here yesterday.'

Murray's shaggy brows snapped together. 'Interfering busybody of a woman!'

'It's her job to interfere. She's trying to get you well. We all thought it was what you wanted too.' Lisle looked at him steadily. 'Who were all these people, anyway?'

He shrugged defensively. 'Advisers in various capacities. I'm not in charge at Harlow Bannerman any more, but I do have other things in the pipeline which have been neglected while I've been lying here.'

'Then they should stay neglected. You need *rest*.'

He gave a satisfied smile. 'And now I shall have it. I've dealt with the outstanding matters. All I need to do now is get strong for the wedding.' He studied her face. 'Perhaps you should do the same. You looked like a ghost when you came in just now. I want to see you looking radiant.'

'If I use all my radiance now, I'll have none left for the wedding.' Lisle made herself smile. 'Jake tells me his mother is coming to England very soon. I thought I'd invite her to stay at the Priory.'

'Splendid,' Murray approved. 'She'll be company for you.'

Will she? Lisle wondered ironically. The prospect of the visit was an alarming one, and she was taking nothing for granted. She had little doubt that Mrs Allard would have found the suddenness of her son's decision to marry puzzling at the very least.

The days went past slowly, with Lisle trapped between boredom and loneliness. There were a couple of guarded phone calls from Gerard which confirmed that Harlow Bannerman was being turned inside out and upside down. He sounded depressed and even a little hostile, so she forbore to press him for details. And he never mentioned Carla Foxton, so perhaps that affair was a thing of the past—or so Lisle fervently hoped. She had wondered once or twice whether she should have passed on to Gerard Jake's words of warning, but on balance had decided against it. There was little doubt in her mind that the covert hostility she had sensed was aimed at Jake, whom her brother regarded as the author of most of his wrongs.

Oliver Grayson had telephoned too, but Lisle had been out for a walk when his call came through, and she decided not to return it. It seemed safer on a number of counts, she thought wryly, remembering a time when safety had not mattered.

But it wasn't only Harlow Bannerman which had been turned inside out and upside down. . . .

Each day she waited for Jake to ring, and when no call came she remained on tenterhooks until evening, waiting for the car to appear. Only it didn't.

At least he found the time to phone the hospital each day, she discovered. Murray relayed odd pieces of information with evident satisfaction, obviously assuming that she and Jake were constantly in touch. Lisle didn't disillusion him. He was taking his enforced leisure more easily now, and there was even an air of satisfaction about him which might be because the consultant in charge of his case had intimated he might be allowed home fairly soon.

And once he was home, there would be no earthly reason for the wedding to be delayed, Lisle thought, her heart thudding in a strange sick mixture of excitement and panic. That was, of course, if there was going to be a wedding. Perhaps the prolonged silence was an indication that Jake was having second thoughts, but was reluctant to announce his decision before Murray was completely restored to health. Her own feelings, of course, wouldn't count, because she wasn't supposed to have any, unless it was pique and a mercenary regret that she had allowed a rich man to slip through her fingers.

It wasn't a train of thought conducive to a tranquil mind and restful nights, but then she had relinquished all hope of either almost from the first moment that Jake had entered her life.

She was working off some excess spleen by pruning the roses to within an inch of their lives when Mrs Peterson came to tell her that Mr Allard's office wanted to speak to her on the phone.

She flew into the house, only to be brought down to earth with a bang when she heard Mrs Pearce's friendly tones greeting her.

'How are you, Miss Bannerman? Mr Allard has had to go to the States, but he wanted to let you know that his mother will be here on Tuesday, and will be holding a small dinner party at her hotel in the evening. He hopes you haven't already made arrangements for that night.'

There had been a time, Lisle thought, when her engagement diary had been crammed for weeks ahead. It probably could be again, if only that was what she wanted.

She said in a small wooden voice, 'No, that will be fine. What hotel is Mrs Allard staying at?'

Mrs Pearce gave her the information, but Lisle could hear the note of surprise in her voice. Presumably she had been expected to know where her future mother-in-law was staying.

Later Lisle telephoned Janie and arranged to change and afterwards sleep at the flat on Tuesday.

'You can even collapse if you want to,' Janie's voice lilted along the line. 'What's Mamma like? Very formidable?'

Lisle stared through the library window at a leafless shrub.

'I don't know,' she admitted wearily. 'I suppose time alone will show.'

'Of course, I keep forgetting that this isn't exactly a conventional courtship,' said Janie. 'Under normal circumstances, you'd be on terms with all his family and friends by now.' She paused. 'He must be very busy. Graham said today that Harlow Bannerman share prices are rising nicely, almost rocketing in fact. You're marrying the Midas touch, darling. Aren't you gratified?'

Lisle smiled rather wanly. 'I think my feelings can most accurately be described as mixed.'

By the time Tuesday evening arrived, the mixture had congealed into nervous edginess. She travelled up to London during the afternoon and had her hair done at her favourite salon.

Jake had still not come back from his trip when she had phoned rather apprehensively to tell him she was staying at the flat overnight. She had half expected a return call forbidding her to do any such thing, but none had been forthcoming.

She received a heartening welcome from Janie, who was full of plans for her impending move. The unknown Anita, it seemed, had proved more than amenable.

'Not as glamorous an address as here,' said Janie, looking round with a smile as they drank coffee together in the kitchenette. 'But you can't win them all. And this was wonderful while it lasted—or I always thought so, at least. But I was never too sure about you. It seemed to me that a lot of the time, and particularly during the latter months, you were just— going through the motions. That you'd have been just as happy down at the Priory.'

Lisle stared down at her cup. 'Perhaps,' she said noncommittally.

How odd, she thought, that she and Janie should have lived together for those months, conducting a perfectly amiable but surface relationship, and only now, when they were apart, discovering these perceptions about each other.

She bathed, and wrapped in Janie's dressing gown took a long careful time to apply her cosmetics. She had just finished when there was a long imperative ring at the doorbell.

Lisle stared at herself, seeing her natural colour paling under the dusting of blusher. It had to be Jake, even though he was much too early, and probably angry with her. She opened the door, her heart sinking, and stared incredulously.

'Gerard? My word—what's happened? Has there been an accident?'

Her brother's face seemed a mask of blood, and there were deep stains on his shirt and suit, which was damp and muddy. He was sagging as if his legs wouldn't support him against Oliver Grayson.

'No accident,' said Oliver. 'He isn't too coherent, but it appears he's been mugged. I'd called in at that wine bar near the office, and when I came out I heard a groan and found him lying in the little alley at the side.'

'But he should have gone to a hospital,' Lisle protested, pressing trembling hands to her cheeks.

Oliver shook his head. 'He absolutely refused. Insisted on being brought here, even though I reminded him you were down in the country.'

From behind Lisle, Janie said, 'You'd better bring him in. Put him on the sofa. Lisle, you'd better call his doctor.'

Gerard said suddenly, 'No—not him. Don't want him to see me.'

Oliver guided him into the sitting room, where he collapsed on to the sofa with a faint groan.

Janie bit her lip. 'I'll phone Tom,' she said. Her brother was a houseman at a London teaching hospital. 'If he's not on duty, I know he'll come.' She turned to Gerard. 'Will that be all right? We can clean you up, but we've got to make sure no real damage has been done.'

There was a pause, then a sullen, 'Yes.'

Lisle sank down on the floor beside him and took his hand. 'Poor love—how awful! Did you catch sight of them? Would you know them again?'

Gerard gave a small cracked laugh. 'It was Foxton. He was—waiting for me. He seemed all right at first, then he just swung at me. I—fell down, and he kicked me.'

Lisle shuddered, and there was an expression of deep distaste on Oliver Grayson's face. He glanced at his watch.

'Unless there's anything else I can do, Lisle, I think I'll go. I have an engagement this evening, and I'm going to be late. . . .'

'Yes, of course.' Lisle jumped up. 'I—I can't thank you enough, Oliver. You've been very kind.'

'And you needn't worry.' As she opened the flat door for him, he gave her a wry look. 'Gerard and I have never been friends, but you can rely on my discretion, for your sake if not for his.' He paused and his voice gentled a little. 'Don't look so stricken, my dear. Some angry husband was bound to catch up with him eventually. Perhaps this will teach him a much needed lesson.'

Lisle sighed. 'Perhaps.' She gave him a small smile. 'Thank you again, anyway.'

He said in a low voice, 'I'd do anything for you, Lisle—you know that.' He took her hand, his thumb caressing her skin. 'Are you quite determined to go through with this—marriage? Is there nothing I can say or do to persuade you?'

'Nothing.' Gently but firmly she freed herself. 'Oliver, I'm sorry. I don't need to be reminded of how badly I've behaved towards you . . .'

'That wasn't what I was trying to do,' he said ruefully. 'I'm just telling you, my dear, that if you need an escape route, I'm prepared to provide one.'

She was silent for a long moment. Then she said wearily, 'There is no escape. There can't be.'

He watched her, incredulity deepening in his face. 'You're in love with him? My word!'

'Is it so unbelievable?' she asked unhappily.

'Oh, he's an attractive fellow. I don't think anyone's in any doubt of that,' Oliver said bitterly. 'But, Lisle, he's ruthless! I've never met anyone like him. He cuts through everything like—like a bloody laser beam. These past ten days or so have been a revelation!'

Lisle bent her head. 'You don't have to tell me that,' she muttered.

He touched her hair awkwardly. 'My poor girl—what a hell of a mess! What can Murray have been thinking of, for heaven's sake? He can't have been under any illusion about Allard, and if he wanted his successor in the company to be a hatchet man, who can blame him? We needed shaking up, and more. But to involve you. . . .' He sighed heavily.

She didn't look at him. 'Yet I love him. I—I didn't want to, or expect to. But it happened, and there's not a thing I can do about it. I don't expect you to understand, Oliver. . . .'

He said gently, 'Perhaps I understand better than you think. Goodnight, my dear.'

Lisle went slowly back into the flat and closed the door, her face sober.

In the sitting room, Janie was dabbing the blood from Gerard's face with swabs of cotton wool dipped in warm water and Savlon.

She looked at Lisle and said calmly, 'It looks gruesome, but I think it's mainly a nosebleed. Oh, and he seems to have a broken tooth. But Tom's on his way, and we'll know better then. They're just about the same size, so I've asked him to bring some spare jeans and a sweater,' she added practically.

Lisle came to her side. 'Janie, let me do that.'

'No, it's all right.' Janie gave a small, taut smile as Gerard winced and muttered something under his breath. 'I can manage until Tom arrives. Besides, you need to get ready. Jake will be here at any moment and he'll expect you to be ready.'

'Allard coming here?' Gerard twisted, grimacing. His nose was badly swollen, and his lip was cut, possibly on the broken tooth, Lisle thought, but he was beginning to look more normal. 'Oh, that's all I need! I don't want to see him. He's not to know about all this—do you hear?'

Lisle said wearily, 'Yes, I hear, although I promise you it wouldn't come as any great surprise to him. I'll go and get ready at once, so there'll be no excuse for us to hang around when he arrives.'

The dress she had decided to wear wasn't new, but it was a favourite of hers, one that she felt relaxed and happy in, and it seemed quite important to hang on to all the relaxation and happiness that she could get.

It was made of cream wool as light and soft as a cobweb in a delicate crochet design with a tiny ruffled neck, and long sleeves, and glamorised by an unobtrusive glitter of gold among the threads. She put small golden roses in her ears, her only other jewellery being her engagement ring. She was just spraying on scent when the doorbell rang again.

She snatched up the dress's matching shawl and went to the door, her gold kid purse clutched in her other hand.

In evening dress, Jake looked taller than ever, and her heart turned over at the sight of him.

There was an extra tinge of colour in her face, as she remembered their last encounter, and her eyes were shy as they met his. He was probably remembering too, which explained the cool constraint in his voice as he greeted her.

'I'm ready.' Lisle touched her lips nervously with the tip of her tongue.

'So I see.' His face was derisive. 'Very demure, beauty, but rather out of character. Who are you trying to fool?'

She stifled the hurt, shrugging slightly. 'Not you, of course, but presumably your mother could still have some illusions.'

'Not many.' His hard mouth smiled, but his eyes did not. They were almost silver this evening. As cold and glittering as frost, she thought. 'No offers of coffee this evening. No civilised sherry?'

'I didn't think we had time.' She tried to sound casual. 'Shouldn't we be going?' It had occurred to her that they might bump into Tom on the stairs and that he, in his innocence, would give the whole game away.

'Just as you wish.' Jake held the door open so that she could precede him into the corridor outside.

They were in the car and already drawing away from the kerb when Tom's elderly car came round the corner. He saw her, and gave her a cheerful 'thumbs-up' and she waved in reply before sitting back in her seat with a concealed sigh of relief. Tom was pleasant and capable, and if Gerard needed even minor treatment, he would cope.

'Another friend of yours?' Jake's voice bit at her.

'Janie's brother. He's a doctor.'

'Does he usually make house calls at this hour?'

'He visits his sister quite regularly,' Lisle returned coolly, and closed her ears to whatever it was he muttered under his breath.

After a pause, she said, 'I expect you're wondering how it is I'm back at the flat. . . .'

'No. I've discovered that it's best not to enquire too closely into your motives for anything,' he said icily.

Lisle drew a breath. 'Then I won't attempt to explain.'

'I doubt if you could.' There was a sudden odd hoarseness in his tone, a suggestion of anger damped down, but threatening to flare again violently which was disturbing. She knew he didn't like her being at the flat, but surely this was an overreaction. Or was this what she could expect whenever she disregarded one of his

wishes? she wondered wryly. After a silence, he went
on, 'But we won't discuss it now. My mother will be
expecting us to present at least a semblance of amity,
and I don't want to disappoint her.'

She was chilled. She hadn't expected lovemaking or
even tender words, aware that she herself had quite
deliberately strangled any prospect of that, but she hadn't
bargained for his icy grimness either.

Oh dear, she thought miserably. What hope was
there for a relationship which united love on one side
with mistrust on the other? And knew with a kind of
despair that the answer was—none.

CHAPTER EIGHT

LISLE felt mentally frozen when eventually they arrived at the hotel where Mrs Allard had her suite. They hadn't spoken a word to each other for the remainder of the journey, and Jake's profile, as she stole a sidelong glance, looked as relentless as granite. The evening had hardly begun, but already it was a nightmare, and she was too unnerved by what had happened to Gerard to be certain she could cope.

Jake's mother was a tall woman, very dark like her son, her hair liberally and attractively streaked with grey. There were deep laughter lines round her eyes and mouth, and she was wearing a very expensive amber silk dress as casually as if it was a rag.

As Jake ushered Lisle into the room, she came forward at once to greet them, but her smile was formal and rather muted. She shook hands and said the right things, but the underlying warmth which should have been there was absent, Lisle sensed.

In the circumstances it was a relief to find the evening was not to be a threesome. There were others waiting to be introduced—a cousin of Mrs Allard's, plump and pleasant with a husband to match, Jake's godparents, both university lecturers, and a tall thickset man with glasses who turned out to be the American Director of Allard International's United States operation, who had accompanied Jake back to Britain from his recent trip.

His name was Clement Sorensen, and Lisle found him amazingly easy to talk to, which, she supposed drily, was part of his stock in trade, but nonetheless welcome. On the other hand, conversation with him tended to be slightly embarrassing after a while, because he obviously credited her with more knowledge about the inside workings of Allard International and Harlow Bannerman than she actually possessed, and she guessed he was too shrewd not to realise this, and wonder.

Champagne was served, and Mrs Allard made a little speech, welcoming Lisle as Jake's future wife, after which toasts were drunk, and there was a lot of laughter and banter. Jake joined in it too, standing with his arm round Lisle's shoulders, and only she knew just how impersonal his touch really was—just like a stranger's. She smiled too, and prayed that no one looked into her eyes.

It should have been a wonderful evening. They went down to the restaurant and ate a delicious meal and drank more champagne, and later went to a nightclub where they danced. There were a lot of people there whom she knew, and a constant stream of them came to the table because they had heard about her engagement and wanted to wish her well.

Lisle smiled until her face felt stiff and sore and wished they would leave her alone. Jake looked as if he was carved from stone, and his mother's expression wavered between astonishment and disapproval.

Lisle wondered how much champagne she would have to drink before she had the courage to ask, 'Mrs Allard, why don't you like me? What have I done?' Probably an entire magnum, she decided, and even then her nerve might fail. Mrs Allard seemed as strong-minded as her son.

She was thankful to her heart when the party began to break up in the early hours. Her head was splitting, not from too much champagne, because she had hardly touched a drop, but from the strain of trying to appear radiant when she felt as if she was breaking apart.

Jake had left his car at the hotel, and they had all driven to the club in taxis, so there was a brief wait in the foyer of the club while the doorman whistled up sufficient cars to take them all to their various destinations.

Lisle made herself approach Jake's mother. 'Mrs Allard, I was wondering if perhaps you'd like to come and stay at the Priory for a day or two. The countryside's a bit bleak and barren at this time of year, but it's still lovely—or at least I think so.'

'Yes, I'm sure you think so.' The dark eyes met hers as coolly as Jake's could have done. 'It's very kind of you, of course, but I'm not altogether sure what my plans are for the remainder of my stay.'

In other words—no, Lisle thought, flushing as she stepped back. Well, the overture had been made, and she didn't see what else she could do.

She made her way to Jake's side and touched his arm. He turned immediately.

'I'm sorry if you've been kept waiting. That's the last of our guests on their way. Clem is staying at the same hotel as my mother, so we can share the next cab.'

Lisle bit her lip. 'Could I go straight back to the flat instead? I—I'm very tired.'

'At this time?' His tone was mocking. 'I thought you were the girl who danced until dawn seven nights a week.'

She shook her head, attempting to smile. Even derision was better than this awful coldness. 'You shouldn't believe what you read in the papers.'

'I don't,' he said. 'Only what I see and hear for myself. All right, then, I'll explain to my mother and Clem, and take you back to the flat.'

'There's really no need,' Lisle protested. 'It's only a short ride from here and. . . .'

'I'm quite well aware where it is,' he said shortly. 'Also that you don't want to take me there, just as you couldn't wait to hustle me away earlier. Why, Lisle? What are you trying to hide?'

'Nothing,' she said. She wasn't even sure if it was true. Tom might have recommended Gerard to stay where he was and rest, and if Jake found him there,

there would be endless recriminations to deal with, probably from both sides. Besides, Gerard had lost so much already. Surely she could protect him in this new and unwelcome vulnerability from Jake's abrasiveness.

'Then there's no reason why I shouldn't go with you.' The grey eyes were implacable, holding her in steely thrall.

'No.' She tried to smile appealingly and failed. 'Except—except that I really am tired. This evening has been something of a strain, and. . . .' She paused helplessly.

'And of course that's the only reason for your fatigue.' The contempt in his voice bewildered her. 'What's the matter, Lisle? Afraid I might make you suffer more of my unwelcome attentions?'

They wouldn't be unwelcome, she thought miserably. It had been a loathsome evening from beginning to end, and she longed quite intensely to creep into his arms and let his warm strong body give her comfort. Even when he was in this strange, harsh mood, wanting him was still an agony inside her.

She made herself shrug. 'Perhaps. You haven't exactly kept your word in the past.'

'Then we make a good pair,' he said. 'You treacherous little temptress.'

He turned and walked away from her. She watched him go, sinking her teeth into her bottom lip, aware of an almost overwhelming impulse to follow, to beg him not to leave her like that but to stay with her—all night if he so chose. But it was too late, and besides, they weren't alone.

Even as she moved, forced herself forward to say goodnight to Clem Sorensen, she saw Mrs Allard watching her curiously, and colour flooded into her face.

Jake's mother disapproved of her already. The last thing she wanted was for her to know how disastrously any hope of a relationship between them had gone awry. Yet she must have noticed Jake's abrupt departure, and already drawn her own conclusions, Lisle thought wretchedly.

Her chin lifted, and veiling her troubled emotions under a surface insouciance, she went through the social forms required of her, not daring to relax until her taxi arrived. Jake put her into it, and she leaned forward, offering her lips to him for the goodnight kiss which convention demanded.

For a long moment he looked at her, his eyes flicking restlessly over the tremulous reddened curve of her mouth.

She said on a little imploring note, 'Jake?'

He stepped back as if she had clawed him with her nails, his hard mouth tightening. He said softly and glacially, 'I think not.'

Lisle huddled back in her seat, willing herself not to cry as he gave the driver the fare and the direction, before turning away without another glance at her.

Janie was still awake when she arrived back at the flat. There was a light showing under her bedroom door, and Lisle knocked lightly and went in. Janie was propped up on her pillows, reading, a pair of large horn-rimmed glasses perched on her nose.

'How did it go?' She put her book down.

'Don't ask.' Lisle sat down on the edge of the bed, tracing the pattern on the quilt with a restless finger. 'What did Tom say about Gerard?'

'He's not going to be a pretty sight for a day or two, and he needs a visit to his dentist, but apart from that there's no real harm done.' Janie hesitated. 'We—we didn't tell him what had really happened. Just that Gerard had had a fall. He—Tom, that is—took him back to his place for the night, just to be on the safe side,' she added on a note of constraint.

Lisle said awkwardly, 'Janie, I'm sorry. I can't imagine what prompted Gerard to come here. He knows damned well I'm not living here any more, and

he hadn't the faintest idea I'd be here this evening. I
don't know what he was thinking of.'

Janie gave her an ironic look. 'Don't apologise. I
know all those things, and so did he, and yet he still
comes here. He came to—me, Lisle, and I've got to take
heart from that, even if it makes me the fool of the
century.' She gave a taut smile. 'I'm not telling you
anything you hadn't already guessed, I'm sure.'

'No.' Lisle admitted softly. 'But, Janie. . . .'

'Oh, I know exactly how it all came about. I've
known about Carla Foxton, and all the other ladies
who preceded her, and it makes no difference. I only
wish it did.' Janie's tone was bitter. 'He's lucky Harry
Foxton didn't kill him, and I think he knows it,
although whether it will make any difference to his way
of life in the long term remains to be seen. He's grateful
to me at the moment, and a little ashamed of himself,
but that may not last.'

Lisle studied her in silence. At least Janie was being
realistic, and that might be her saving grace, because
although Gerard might have had a fright, she wondered
whether it would have been a sufficient shock to make
him deviate from the course he had pursued enjoyably
through life.

He was a lightweight, she thought sadly, and
probably always would be, and Janie undoubtedly
deserved better.

'By the way,' Janie said, 'I should warn you that for
reasons best known to himself, he's started to blame
Jake for what happened to him tonight. Apparently
Carla ditched him when she heard about the shake-up
at Harlow Bannerman, and then made a tearful
confession to her husband in order to save her own skin.
Gerard feels that if he was still Sales Director in the
company, none of it would have happened.'

'Then he's fooling himself.' Lisle shook her head. 'As
a matter of fact Jake warned me not long ago that
Harry Foxton was becoming suspicious. I'd have passed

the warning on if I thought it would have been welcome, but in the circumstances I thought it was best to say nothing.' She sighed. 'Now I'm not so sure.'

'No, I think you were right,' Janie said steadily. 'It's Gerard's misfortune that the man who's been placed in control of the company has power, as well as sexual charisma. It's a combination he envies, but he has to learn to cope with it, to come to terms in some way with the fact that Jake Allard is probably twice the man he'll ever be.'

'You think that? Then how . . .?'

'How do I love him?' Janie gave a crooked smile. 'I've asked myself that on many occasions. But you of all people should understand, Lisle. We can't legislate for these things. They—just happen.'

'Yes,' said Lisle, after a long pause. 'They—happen.' She leaned forward and kissed her friend lightly on the cheek, then went to her own room.

But it was a long, bitter time before she could sleep.

Murray was full of eager questions when she visited the hospital the following day. Naturally he wanted to know all about the dinner party, and what she thought of Jake's mother.

'She seems charming,' Lisle assured him, infusing her voice with false enthusiasm. 'And very attractive too.'

He gave a satisfied smile. 'I hoped you'd like each other. You've been so long without a mother's care, my darling. It would be wonderful if Mrs Allard could fill this gap in your life. The fact that she lives in the South of France could be a problem,' he added with a slight frown. 'But perhaps when the grandchildren start to arrive, she'll come back to this country.

'You're impossible!' Lisle scolded. 'You must stop trying to manipulate people.'

His eyes kindled. 'Well, I've made a pretty fair job of it so far, as you should be the first to admit.'

Should I? she thought despairingly. Oh, Murray, if you only knew!

She turned the subject fairly adroitly, discussing plans for his return home, avoiding all mention of her relationship with Jake, or the wedding.

He seemed so much better, so much stronger, she thought as she drove home to the Priory. Surely there would come a time when she could break the news to him that the marriage he had built his hopes on should not and could not take place.

As Lisle brought the Mini to a halt, she saw there was already a car parked in front of the house. She didn't recognise the make or the number, she thought, frowning a little as she left her own vehicle.

She was frankly amazed when a uniformed driver climbed out, and opening one of the rear passenger doors, assisted Mrs Allard to alight.

She gave Lisle a faint smile. 'Hello, I thought I'd take you up on your invitation after all, but if it's not convenient, then you must tell me.'

'It's perfectly convenient,' said Lisle. 'Only I just didn't expect. . . .'

'To see me again,' Mrs Allard supplied wryly. 'Well, I gave you every justification, I must admit.'

Lisle felt more and more bewildered. 'If you'd like to come in, I'll ask the housekeeper to get us some tea.'

'There's no hurry for that.' Mrs Allard gestured around her. 'Wouldn't you like to show me the grounds first? You were quite right about the countryside.'

Lisle felt as if she was in a dream as she obeyed the older woman's suggestion. And as Mrs Allard asked her questions about the layout of the garden, and the various plants and shrubs which had been planted to give life and colour to a normally rather dead time of year, the first awkwardness began to pass.

It was obvious that the older woman was herself a keen gardener. She chatted with animation about her villa, and the different demands in terms of soil and landscape that its grounds made on her.

'But of course you'll see that for yourself when Jake

brings you to visit me, as I hope he will,' she added almost casually. 'I'd thought of taking myself elsewhere and offering you both the place for a honeymoon if I could have persuaded Jake to postpone your marriage until the spring, but he's quite adamant that it must take place as soon as possible.'

'Is he?' Lisle's tone held irony, and Mrs Allard smiled a little.

'Perhaps this is the moment to explain what I'm doing here,' she said. 'For a number of reasons, I'd decided prior to last night that you were not the right wife for my son, and I came to England frankly to do anything I could to stop the business going any further. But—last night—I saw you looking at him when you didn't know you were observed, and it occurred to me that you might love him, and that I could be misjudging you entirely. Am I right?'

Lisle's face felt rigid. 'I don't think you have any right to question me,' she said at last.

'No right? I'm Jake's mother, and I happen to love him too.'

'No one would doubt that, but I assure you that my feelings are really of no concern. I have no intention of marrying Jake.'

'I see.' Mrs Allard was silent for a moment. Then she said drily, 'That's not the impression I have from him. In fact from the scant information he's given me, I gathered you have very little choice in the matter.'

'There's always a choice,' said Lisle. 'My grandfather is making marvellous progress, and he'll be strong enough very soon for me to tell him the truth—that I can't bring myself to go through with it.'

'But can you really do that?' Mrs Allard frowned. 'From what Jake told me, I thought. . . .'

'No matter what he said, there's no obligation—none.' Lisle took a deep breath. 'I may have been living in a crazy dream, but I'm awake now. It's over.'

'You sound as if you're trying to convince yourself.'

Mrs Allard's voice was dry. 'But are you sure it's possible to act as you plan to do?'

'You mean that Jake won't appreciate being jilted?' Lisle asked. 'Well, it doesn't have to be like that. He can be the one to do the jilting if his male pride demands it. But I don't think he'll care particularly— not as long as he can be rid of me.' Her voice broke a little.

'So you do care.' It was a statement, not a question.

Lisle turned her head away, 'It doesn't matter,' she said wearily. 'Mrs Allard, it was kind of you to come here today, but I don't think your visit has achieved anything, unless it's to reassure you that I have no intention of marrying your son.' She swallowed. 'You said you had—reasons for not wanting it. Well, I'm sure they're perfectly valid ones.'

'They seemed so. As soon as your engagement was announced, I began to get phone calls from all kinds of people, all of them with bad news, or so it seemed. I already knew from Jake that you were Murray Bannerman's granddaughter, and that marriage with you was part of the deal he'd agreed with your grandfather. I was naturally horrified. I begged him to reconsider, but he said it was too late. And then the calls started, many of them from friends who were genuinely concerned. They said you were fairly— notorious, that your brother was an inveterate womaniser, and there was little reason to believe you were any less promiscuous. They said you'd lived high, even though the company couldn't afford it, that Harlow Bannerman was nearly bankrupt because of you both. That to save yourself from ultimate penury you'd persuaded your grandfather to buy you a rich husband with the only asset he had left—the company. They said you were mercenary and heartless.' She paused.

Lisle said, 'Oh no,' very softly. 'No wonder you behaved as you did last night!'

'I was prepared to give you the benefit of the doubt,
however. I couldn't imagine Jake selling himself to
anyone remotely resembling the description I'd been
given of you. But when I arrived, I saw for myself how
unhappy he was, how sick at heart.' Mrs Allard sighed.
'I'd never seen him like that before, I was shocked. It
convinced me that everything I'd heard could only be
true.' She smiled sadly. 'I found it very easy to hate
you, even though you were far from being what I had
expected, on the surface anyway. You were younger,
and not as hardboiled as I'd imagined, so I began to
wonder, and then I saw you look at him and realised I'd
made a mistake. Please don't ask me to believe I've
made yet another,' she added.

Lisle bit her lip. She said in a low voice, 'I love him.
But I'm not going to marry him. It was madness ever to
think that I would, and I'm going to convince my
grandfather somehow.'

'And what about Jake?' Mrs Allard gave her a
straight look. 'How will you convince him?'

Lisle flushed. 'I don't see a great deal of problem. He
can't have enjoyed having his hand forced in this way.
And I'm the last woman in the world that he'd ever
have chosen for himself.'

Mrs Allard sighed. 'He must have treated you very
badly.'

'It was just—wrong from the start. It never had a
chance.'

'And you're not prepared to give it one?'

'I'm not the only person involved.' Lisle glanced up
at the threatening sky. 'I think it's going to rain. Shall
we return to the house and have that tea?'

'Yes, that would be very nice.' Mrs Allard didn't look
particularly happy, and the smile she gave Lisle was a
little bleak.

On the way back to the house, Lisle was careful to
keep the conversation to general topics. Mrs Allard's
forthrightness had flustered her because it was so

entirely unexpected. They would probably never meet
again, she thought, and this was a matter of regret to
her, because it now seemed possible that in other
circumstances they could have become friends.

As they turned the corner which led to the front of
the house, Mrs Peterson came rushing to meet them,
her usual placidity in rags, her face white and her eyes
filled with tears.

'Miss Lisle—oh, Miss Lisle! The telephone—it's the
hospital! Oh, Miss Lisle, dear. . . .'

Lisle sprinted for the open front door. Her mouth
was dry and her heart pounding as she stumbled into
the library and snatched up the receiver.

The voice at the other end was kind but rather
remote. It said that Murray had suffered a sudden, severe
collapse and that although resuscitation techniques
had been used, attempts to revive him had not been
successful. This was deeply regretted.

She stared numbly down at the surface of the desk,
her finger tracing a pattern on the tooling of the leather.
It seemed incredibly important that she should do this,
that she should follow every whirl and convolution to
its beginning, because otherwise some disaster might
befall. . . . Some disaster.

She made some reply to the remote voice and
fumbled to replace the receiver on its rest. It was taken
from her hand, and Mrs Allard's arm came round her
warm and supporting.

She said gently, 'My poor child—come and sit down.
Your housekeeper is bringing some tea.'

Lisle felt freezing cold. She said, 'I don't seem to be
able to stop shaking,' in a voice which hardly resembled
hers at all.

She found she was in the drawing room on the sofa,
staring into the fire. The tea had been brought in by a
quietly weeping Mrs Peterson and Jake's mother was
busying herself with the cups.

Lisle said, half to herself, 'But he was better. He was

getting well. He was coming home very soon.'

Mrs Allard gave her a sympathetic look. 'I'm afraid it happens like that sometimes, dear. I'm sure they did all they could.'

'Yes.' Lisle paused, then said huskily, 'I—I have to be glad in a way. Those—machines. He hated them so. He wouldn't have wanted. . . .'

'No,' Mrs Allard's hand closed comfortingly over hers, 'I'm sure he wouldn't. Now, is there anything I can do for you? Your brother will have to be told, of course.'

'Yes, but I'd better do that.' Lisle put down her cup. 'In fact, I'd better do it now.'

'And then I'll telephone Jake,' his mother said. Her eyes met Lisle's. 'He has a right to know too, you know.'

'Yes—yes, of course. I'd be very grateful,' Lisle stammered.

She went into the library and closed the door behind her as she tried to collect her thoughts. There was little point in trying to find Gerard at Harlow Bannerman, she realised. He wouldn't be going near the place until his swollen face had subsided. If he wasn't at the dentist, he would probably be at his flat.

The phone rang and rang, but there was no reply. She would have to try again later, she thought with a sigh. She wished Gerard had been there. She needed to talk to him, to share her bewilderment and the first painful beginnings of grief. He would understand. He had loved Murray too, although not as much as she had. Gerard would comfort her, she told herself with a kind of frantic emphasis.

Her mouth trembled, and she caught at the edge of the desk, allowing the hard wood to bite into her hands. She was fooling herself. All Gerard's sympathy would be reserved for himself, just as it always had been. He had been thinking of the effect of Murray's death on Harlow Bannerman, and in consequence, to himself.

It was Jake she needed to shelter her while he took charge of everything. It was Jake, and only Jake that she wanted, but he was lost to her forever now. Murray's death had released them both from all obligation to each other.

They were free at last, and the thought left her desolate and shaking, because for all her brave words and good intentions that wasn't what she wanted at all. She had spoken to Mrs Allard about crazy dreams, and she wanted them to go on because reality could only be cold and bleak and lonely by contrast. The life she had planned, living quietly in this house, seemed unthinkable—unbearable suddenly.

She folded her arms round her body, shuddering. Utter loneliness or marriage to a man who despised her—that was her choice, and she cringed from either alternative.

She was roused from her unhappy reverie by the unexpected sound of a car on the drive outside. For a moment, she thought it might be Gerard come to lick his wounds in the peace and safety of the Priory, and braced herself as she went out into the hall. To hear that Murray was dead was one thing. To have to acknowledge it verbally as she broke the news to her brother was something else again. She stood, watching the front door, waiting for it to open, as she summoned her strength and her courage.

The door opened and Jake strode in, impatiently shaking the raindrops from his hair and shoulders.

He saw her at once, his brows flying together questioningly as he assimilated her white face and swimming eyes.

'What the hell's happened?' he demanded roughly. 'Has something—someone upset you? I suppose that's my mother's car outside. I had a message to say she was coming down here, and she'd left before I could stop her. . . .'

She said, 'It's Murray.'

His head went back sharply, and he stared at her for a long moment, expelling his breath on a deep sigh.

He said softly and wearily, 'I was afraid of this all along.' His tone became brisker. 'You'd better go and sit down before you collapse. I'm here now, I'll see to everything. You don't have to worry any more.'

Lisle could almost have laughed at that. Her teeth bit painfully into her lower lip. 'Thank you. You're being very—kind. And so has your mother. She was on the point of calling you—asking you to come here.'

'I'm sure she was.' The corner of his mouth twisted. 'Because you certainly wouldn't have done so, would you, Lisle?'

She looked at him, her green eyes stricken and he made an impatient gesture. 'I'm sorry. This is hardly an appropriate time to touch on our personal difficulties. . . .'

'On the contrary,' said Lisle, her glance sliding away to the floor. 'In a way it's the perfect opportunity to—to assure you that this—this engagement need not proceed any further. In fact, I'd like it to stop here and now.'

Jake was silent, the grey eyes narrowed and incredulous as he surveyed her. He said, 'You don't know what you're saying.'

'Oh, but I do,' she said huskily. 'We made an agreement for Murray's sake, and that alone. His— passing renders it null and void.' She tugged at the big diamond, coaxing it from her finger, and held it out to him.

He made no move to take it. He said quietly, 'I don't think this is a time for hasty decisions. You're overwrought and you need time to think.'

'I've had a lot of time to think. I've done little else since the night we met,' said Lisle. She wanted very much to sink down on to the hall floor and weep, but she dared not display any sign of weakness. She had to make him believe her. 'You can't pretend that you want this—this sterile bargain we made to continue now that the reason for it no longer exists.'

For a moment she thought she saw him wince, but when he spoke his voice was so impassive, she realised it must have been some trick of the fading light.

'No, I won't pretend that, Lisle, but had it occurred to you that the fulfilment of Murray's wishes may not be so easy to avoid. He was more determined than perhaps you think.'

'But I am equally determined.' She put the ring down on the table outside the drawing room door. 'Your—your mother's in there. I'll ask Mrs Peterson to bring fresh tea, and then I'm going to my room for a while. I'd like to be alone.'

For a moment she thought he was going to move forward, take her in his arms, and her whole body tensed as if warding off a blow. By the grim hardening of his mouth, she knew he had registered her instinctive reaction.

But all he said with cool civility was, 'Just as you wish.'

I wish, Lisle thought as she turned away to go in search of Mrs Peterson, I wish that you loved me, and that I could cry all this out in your arms. I wish that you were my lover so that I could wake next to you tomorrow, and know that I would never be lonely again.

She returned to the hall on her way back from the kitchen quarters. It was empty, but she could hear the murmur of voices from behind the closed drawing room door.

Her ring had vanished from the table, and as she went slowly upstairs, it occurred to her how bare her hand looked without it.

As bare and empty as the days, weeks and months which stretched ahead of her now—without Jake.

CHAPTER NINE

THE funeral was over at last. The house had been crammed with people all wishing to pay their last respects, but they were leaving now, and Lisle was thankful that the end of this particular ordeal was in sight.

It was a raw day, and Gerard had advised her to remain by the fire while he saw the last remaining guests off the premises. When he returned, she supposed they would adjourn to the library for the reading of the will, although strictly that was a formality as she already knew its contents.

And after that, she would have to try and make some plans.

It had been impossible over the last days to give any thought to the future. There had been all the legalities and rituals of death to conform with, although Jake had been a tower of strength where these were concerned. There had been telephone calls to make and answer and letters of condolence to reply to, and in a way she had been grateful for the calls on her time and attention that these activities made, because they prevented her thinking. . . .

She was bitterly ashamed because she couldn't be sure how many of the tears she had wept were for Murray, and how many for herself, for her loneliness and uncertainty. She couldn't even grieve unselfishly for the grandfather she had loved, she thought wretchedly.

Jake had not said a word more on the subject of their broken engagement, and she had to be grateful for this, but then, if she was honest, he had said very little at all of a personal nature to her. He had been kind and considerate, but aloof, the grey eyes shuttered and enigmatic when he looked at her.

155

Mrs Allard had noticed the missing ring immediately, but she had said nothing, although her face was frankly concerned. She had stayed at the Priory overnight, and rather to her surprise, Lisle had found that her presence had eased the situation between herself and Jake. By the time his mother departed, he had withdrawn behind the barrier of cool courtesy to which Lisle was slowly becoming accustomed.

She had traced Gerard at last, finding him during the evening at her old flat with Janie again. Her news was clearly a blow to him, but it had been a couple of days before he had come down to the Priory—a fact on which Jake had commented caustically.

'I didn't realise he was so vain,' he said coldly when another twenty-four hours had passed, and there was still no sign of Gerard.

'He isn't well.' Lisle had leapt to Gerard's defence, and Jake's mouth curled in contempt.

'No? Then he'll have to learn to keep away from other men's wives. Or was he trying to keep it secret that Harry Foxton gave him a going over? If so, he's been wasting his time. Foxton was trumpeting it all over London the following day—as a warning to any other potentially interested parties, no doubt,' he added sardonically.

'Oh.' Lisle flushed, mortified. 'He—he didn't want you to know.'

'Why not? Afraid of forfeiting my good opinion? Surely not.' He stopped abruptly, his eyes flicking over her distressed face, and he sighed. 'I'm sorry, I have no right to punish you for Gerard's shortcomings.' He paused. 'In fact, I've no right to punish you at all. Forgive me.'

It had been, she thought wryly, almost the only intimate moment they had shared.

Each night, she had walked the floor in her room, fighting a compulsion to go to him, to offer herself on any terms at all. But fear prevented her. Fear that he would look at her with those blank polite eyes and reject her. She sighed. Any such move on her part could only be an embarrassment to him, and a humiliation for her.

He might have wanted her once, she told herself, but no longer. And it was obvious that her decision to end their travesty of a relationship had been a relief to him. His whole attitude emphasised that.

A log subsided in a little shower of sparks in the wide grate, and Lisle knelt to make up the fire, aware of a chill that had little to do with the temperature of the room.

The drawing room door opened, and Gerard came in looking peevish.

'Well, that's the last of them, thank goodness. I thought Oliver Grayson would never go.' He shot her a malicious glance. 'Hoping for a private *tête-à-tête* with you, no doubt.'

'You think so?' Lisle dusted her hands together and rose to her feet. 'Now, I had the distinct impression he was avoiding me.'

'Not you, my sweet—your erstwhile fiancé. The rumour at the office is that our Oliver will be resigning before long.'

Lisle paused. Then she said slowly, 'Well, he won't be short of offers from other firms. Grandfather thought very highly of him, you know.'

'Oh yes,' Gerard agreed indifferently. 'But he won't get the same kind of testimonial from Allard, broken engagement or not. Poor Grayson, I hope you haven't wrecked his career along with his hopes.'

She said in a stifled voice, 'So do I. Now I suppose we'd better find Mr Lithgow and get this will business over with. Do you know where he is?'

'Waiting for us in the library, for reasons best known to himself. Perhaps he feels this room is too frivolous for anything as solemn as a will reading.'

Lisle sighed. 'Do we really have to go through with it?

What point is there, after all? We know what the provisions are.'

'I suppose we do.' Gerard gave her an odd look.

'Of course. He told us both a couple of years ago.' Lisle spoke with a trace of impatience. 'You can't have forgotten.'

'I haven't forgotten what he said then,' Gerard agreed. 'But a lot of things have happened since then, Lisle. It's never occurred to you that there might have been some changes? Or didn't you know that old Lithgow had been to the hospital a couple of times at Murray's urgent request?'

'No, I didn't.' Lisle spoke calmly, but she was conscious of the first vague stirrings of alarm. She was remembering the staff's complaints about the frequency of visitors, and Murray's own words when she had questioned him—'*Advisers in various capacities*', delivered with evident satisfaction. She said after another pause, 'Perhaps he wanted to make some kind of bequest to Jake. After all, he—he liked him very much.'

'Yes, didn't he?' Gerard's voice was dry. 'Where is Allard, by the way?'

'I don't know. Probably in his room, packing. His mother is returning to the South of France in a day or two. He'll want to spend some time with her before she goes, and there's nothing more for him to stay here for.'

Gerard gave her a startled look. 'I doubt if he'd agree with you, my sweet. Apart from any personal legacy, he has a vested interest in Murray's will through you.'

'Not any more.' Lisle held out her bare hand. 'Had you really not noticed? I thought you were just being unusually tactful.'

'Naturally I'd seen the rock was missing, but I'd assumed it was something to do with mourning.' Gerard gave her a horrified look. 'For Pete's sake, Lisle! You haven't done anything drastic, have you?'

'If you choose to put it that way—yes.'

Her brother's voice was sharp. 'Then you're a fool,

my dear. From the hints old Lithgow was dropping to me earlier, it's something you may regret. Now, we'd better go and hear what he has to say.'

Jake was already in the library when they arrived. The dark face was cool and reflective, and Lisle could read nothing from his expression. Mr Lithgow, on the other hand, looked positively harassed.

He began briskly enough. There were a few small bequests, including a generous lump sum to the Petersons, before he arrived at the main provisions. He dealt with Gerard's part of the legacy first, and it was all familiar and straightforward exactly as Murray himself had explained it to them.

She heard her name, and looked at the little solicitor, aware that he had hesitated.

Mr Lithgow cleared his throat. 'I am not sure, Miss Bannerman, whether or not your grandfather took you into his confidence over the recent alterations he saw fit to make in the provisions which affect you. As you know, it was his intention to leave you this house and sufficient money for its upkeep and to provide you with an income, as well as some more personal items. However, in view of your forthcoming marriage, he decided to place more emphasis on the future. The Priory therefore, and the income I have mentioned is now left to you in trust for your children by Mr James Christopher Allard, and the entire bequest is wholly conditional on your marriage with Mr Allard taking place within one calendar month.'

There was a roaring in her ears, and Mr Lithgow and his solemn face seemed suddenly to have receded to a great distance.

She said in a small polite voice like a child's, 'I'm sorry, I don't quite understand.'

Mr Lithgow looked at her with slight disapproval. 'My explanation lacked clarity? Then I had better read the terms to you as they are set out here.'

The dry legal language was no easier to comprehend,

but it gave her a breathing space and served as well to convince her that it was all terribly, horrifyingly true.

When he had finished reading, she said, 'And if Mr Allard and I fail to—comply—what then?'

Mr Lithgow rustled his papers, clearly embarrassed. 'Various charities benefit from both the sale of the house, and the monies which would have come to you.'

She felt numb. 'In other words, I get nothing.' She was aware that Jake was watching her, the grey eyes enigmatic.

'On the contrary, Miss Bannerman.' Mr Lithgow sounded almost shocked. 'I cannot see where the problem arises. You and Mr Allard are, after all, engaged, and I understood from my late client that your marriage would soon take place. All that has happened is that your inheritance has been placed in trust for your children.' He gave her a benign smile. 'As I'm sure you know, Miss Bannerman, your marriage was one of the dearest wishes of your grandfather's heart, and there is no reason why matters should not proceed to everyone's entire satisfaction.'

From the other side of the room—or possibly from the other side of the known world—she heard Jake say shortly, 'No reason at all. Thank you, Mr Lithgow, for explaining Mr Bannerman's wishes so clearly. Can we persuade you to stay and have some lunch with us?'

Mr Lithgow looked gratified as he gathered his papers together and stowed them in his briefcase. 'I am very much obliged, but I fear that I must return to the office. I have various appointments of some urgency.'

Somehow Lisle found herself shaking hands, even managing a smile. As Gerard and Jake escorted Mr Lithgow out of the room, she sank limply back into her chair, staring blindly in front of her.

Gerard was the first to return. 'So, my sweet, you're a blushing bride once more.'

Lisle looked at him. 'You knew!'

He shook his head. 'Not the details, but I guessed he'd find some way of backing you into a corner. Murray was never a trusting soul, heaven knows, and he probably guessed your engagement would survive no longer than he did himself.'

She said fiercely, 'How could he do such a thing? How could he?'

Gerard shrugged. 'To make sure he got what he wanted, as he always did. He was a determined man, and he wouldn't allow a little thing like his own death to interfere with his plans for the human race, or his section of it.' He gave a short laugh. 'Your only problem now is to convince the hard-headed Mr Allard that you've had a romantic change of heart, totally unprompted by any mercenary motivation. I wish you luck.'

She got up restlessly and went over to the window. 'I—I could always contest the will.'

'On what grounds? That Murray was of unsound mind when he made it?' Gerard's mouth turned down at the corners. 'That simply wouldn't wash, darling. He was knife-sharp to the end, and you know it, and so does anyone else who had any dealings with him.' He gave a slight yawn. 'No, I'm afraid, sister dear, you'll have to give in gracefully to the inevitable—which in your case is Jake Allard. Use your powers of persuasion, and that pretty bauble will be back in your finger before you know it.'

'I can't. I'd rather die!'

'Brave words.' His voice was sceptical. 'But you can't bluff any more, Lisle. The pistol at your head is really loaded this time, and one has to be practical, after all.'

'Yes,' Jake said evenly from the doorway, 'one certainly does.'

Lisle stayed where she was, her back turned rigidly to him. Her heart was thudding so hard suddenly that she felt almost sick. She felt rather than saw a movement and realised that Gerard was discreetly making himself scarce.

She waited for Jake to say something, but the silence in the room seemed to go on for ever. She began to ache with tension, her jaw set, her hands clenching into fists among the folds of her black dress.

She was just beginning to think she might scream when he said silkily, 'What are you waiting for, beauty? A declaration of undying passion, made on my knees?'

Lisle gritted her teeth. 'Hardly.'

'Then let's follow your brother's advice and stick to practicalities. Unless we comply with your grandfather's requirements, you'll be homeless and virtually penniless.' His voice was curt. 'Do you agree that's an accurate assessment of the position?'

Lisle stared unseeingly at the garden. 'I could get a job. I'm not helpless.'

'No, but you're totally unqualified. You're unlikely to be offered anything which will bring in half the salary you were paid from Harlow Bannerman, if in fact you can find work at all.'

Her voice sounded brittle. 'I'm well aware it's a buyer's market.'

'It is indeed.' His tone was quiet and emotionless. 'You won't get a better offer than mine, Lisle, on economic grounds alone.'

She lifted one shoulder in a shrug. 'And what other grounds could there be?'

'None at all,' he said. 'Murray has put us into a cleft stick, beauty. We no longer have a choice. Little as either of us wants this marriage, we have to go through with it. But it doesn't have to be a life sentence. Murray imposed no conditions about us having to stay married.'

Anguish stabbed at her, but she managed to control her instinctive recoil from his words.

She said, 'You make it sound so simple. But it isn't. There are—other conditions, in case you'd forgotten.'

'You mean Murray's flattering faith in our ability to have children? I don't know of any reason why we shouldn't.'

'No—except that I wouldn't want. . . .' Her hands were clasped in front of her now as if she was praying.

'What wouldn't you want?' His voice bit at her.

'To bring a child into something that wasn't a real home,' she said baldly. 'And ours couldn't be—not if it was just a temporary measure to satisfy a legal requirement.'

There was a silence, then he said, 'That's a fair point. Will it reassure you if I promise that any marriage between us will remain—merely a legal requirement?'

Her voice was a thread of sound. 'I—I don't know. I can't think straight. You must give me time.'

'I seem to have heard that before,' he said drily. 'Very well, Lisle, take as much time as you need—up to a calendar month, of course. In the circumstances, no one will wonder if we keep the actual ceremony as quiet and simple as possible.'

'You're very sure of yourself,' she said bitterly. 'You're convinced that I'm going to agree.'

'I'd like to think you had an alternative,' he said. 'But you love this house, and you've always enjoyed a certain standard of living. I can't visualise you throwing it all away. . . .'

'For a principle?' she said stonily. 'No, that's hardly my style, is it? I'll let you know as soon as I've reached a decision. No doubt you'll want to get back to London now.' She paused. 'Thank you for everything you've done. You've been more than kind.'

'What did it cost you to tell me that, I wonder?' he asked with cold irony. 'Yes, I'm going. Please don't keep me waiting too long for your answer.'

Lisle heard the library door close, and slowly she forced herself to relax the stiff tension of her stance. She had been terrified that Jake might touch her, because that would have been fatal.

Suddenly she knew she couldn't face Gerard's questions. She slipped out of the library, and went upstairs to her room. She sat down on the edge of the bed and tried to make sense of what had happened, but it was impossible. She felt desperately tired, and infinitely wretched.

She tried to imagine living with Jake, sharing a roof with him in a marriage which would be no marriage at all, until he decided it should end. She shivered. It was a horrifying prospect—almost as bad as the thought of never seeing him again, which seemed the only alternative.

The fact that she would be losing her home and the sheltered life she had frankly enjoyed seemed an irrelevance. Nothing mattered except that she loved Jake—and that he, in his turn, could not have expressed his indifference more plainly.

'Little as either of us wants this marriage. . . .' The remembered words stung at her brain.

'But he wanted me,' she thought fiercely. 'I can make him want me again.'

She stared across the room at her mirrored reflection. Worry, sleepless nights and sheer wretchedness had drained most of the colour from her face, and she had dark shadows under her eyes. She gave a little soundless sigh. It was hardly an appropriate time to begin a campaign to attract Jake back to her physically, but what else could she do? Tell him that she loved him? She could imagine his reaction only too well. Gerard's cynical comments flicked at her, but she had to admit he was right. No man in Jake's position was going to believe any such confession.

She had no idea how long she had been sitting there, going over the same ground again and again, trying to find a solution and failing, but the tap on the door made her jump.

She got up, her heart beating quickly and unsteadily, and crossed to open it, wondering, hoping that it might be Jake.

But if was Mrs Peterson, still rather red-eyed, but trying to smile.

'Lunch is served, Miss Lisle.' She paused. 'It's just you, and Mr Gerard. Mr Allard left about twenty minutes ago. He didn't want to disturb you because he thought you were probably resting, but he asked me to give you this.' She handed Lisle an envelope, and turned away.

The envelope weighed heavy in her hand. Wonderingly, Lisle opened it, and the diamond ring slid out and lay in her palm like a world of frozen tears.

She was very quiet during lunch, and if Gerard noticed that she was merely pushing the food round her plate, at least he made none of his edged comments. In fact, he seemed subject to frequent bouts of introspection himself, she thought, stealing a glance at him as Mrs Peterson came to clear the table and bring coffee.

At last he said abruptly, 'I've been thinking, Lisle, that I'd better get back to London myself. There are meetings scheduled which I ought to attend. You could come with me, if you like, and stay at the flat. I shouldn't imagine you'd want to be on your own here just at present.'

She was frankly amazed. Gerard didn't normally show so much consideration, and he had never extended an invitation for her to stay with him before. After only a momentary hesitation, she accepted. She still had letters of condolence to reply to, but that could be done as well from London as the Priory.

She could keep occupied in London too, she thought, and stop thinking for a while. There would be art exhibitions she could visit, quite apart from the growing imminence of Christmas. She could manage some shopping as well.

And Jake was in London too, although with things as they were between them it was difficult to read any kind of advantage into that. She bit her lip at the thought.

And if all else failed, she could always job-hunt, she told herself without a great deal of hope. Or there were training courses she could apply for. She was far from being some kind of brainless idiot. There would be—had to be something she could do.

Apart, of course, from marrying Jake.

When lunch was over, she went upstairs, urged rather impatiently by Gerard and threw a few things into a case. As she worked, she looked around her, wondering how she would feel if the Priory was never to be her home again, and knowing with deep, sobering certainty suddenly that it didn't matter—that nothing mattered except Jake and her love and need for him. That she would give anything if he would love her in return, only now it was impossible. That will—that awful, awful will had been driven like a wedge between them, the very opposite effect, she knew, to that which had been intended.

She whispered silently, 'Oh, Grandfather!' and the dammed-back tears began, slowly at first, and then with agonising swiftness, trickling between the fingers she had pressed childishly to her face, as if hoping to hold back the flood of misery.

She still wasn't entirely sure why she was weeping, but it was a catharsis she had badly needed, and as the last gasping sobs died away, and she was able to dry her eyes and bathe the worst ravages from her face, she realised she was feeling a little better, slightly less confused and bitter.

The flat which Gerard used in London, and which now belonged to him, was in a much older building than Jake's, and was a pleasant mellow place. Gerard reminded her where everything was, and gave her a quick tour of the kitchen cupboards before he went to the office.

Left to herself, Lisle made up the comfortable bed in the spare room with linen she found in the hot cupboard, and brewed herself some coffee, before she tidied up a little. The flat was clean, but rather cluttered, and she wandered about familiarising herself with her surroundings. There were, of course, the inevitable signs of female occupation, including a large flask of perfume in the bathroom. Lisle removed the stopper and gave an experimental sniff, grimacing slightly. It was musky and cloying and not her style at all, although it would probably have suited Carla Foxton beautifully.

She wondered if Gerard missed her very badly. Not a word had been said between them about the end of the affair, or his subsequent beating, but then Jake's presence had been an inhibition.

She remembered Janie's comment that Gerard blamed Jake for the whole sorry business, and told herself that she must have that out with him. They had been civil to each other during the lead-up to the funeral, but no more, and on the few occasions when they had been in each other's company for any length of time, Lisle had sensed tension.

She didn't want them to become great friends—she was sufficiently a realist to know that would probably never be possible—but she felt strongly that they should be able to deal with each other without covert hostility being an element in the relationship.

But when Gerard returned that evening he was in a foul mood, and it was evident from his muttered remarks that Jake was the prime cause of his annoyance. Lisle asked a few casual questions, and discovered that Gerard had been testing, perhaps unwisely, how much weight the Bannerman name still carried in the company, and had been totally dissatisfied by the answers he had received.

'And Grayson is definitely resigning. It's no longer just a rumour,' he told her.

'Oh, I'm sorry.' The old order was changing, and no mistake, she thought rather forlornly.

'And I may join him,' Gerard muttered. 'I've no

intention of being a glorified office boy for very much longer.' He gave a moody laugh. 'Who'd ever have thought that Grayson and I would end up on the same side?'

Lisle said quietly, 'Does it have to be a question of sides? Couldn't you all work together for the good of the company—as Murray wanted?'

'My word, there's a pious thought,' Gerard mocked. 'May I remind you, my sweet, that not all Murray's wishes have had your undivided support? Or don't you count the present little local difficulty?'

She tried to smile. 'I think that's slightly different. What do you want to do about dinner? I looked in the fridge, but there didn't seem to be a great deal. . . .'

'No, there isn't.' Gerard seemed to rouse himself from a temporary abstraction. 'I thought we'd eat out—Italian, maybe.'

'That would be nice,' she said rather flatly. She had been hoping—absurdly, she realised—for some message, however brief from Jake. If, of course, he knew she was in London. The way things were, Gerard might well not have told him. And she jibbed somehow at asking him directly. Gerard was no fool, and any forlorn question of that nature might arouse his suspicions about the true state of her feelings.

When two days had passed without a word from Jake, she was sure Gerard had said nothing to him. But at the same time, she told herself that if he had taken the trouble to phone the Priory, Mrs Peterson would have told him where she was. It seemed he had not done so, and the neglect chilled her.

Although it should not have done. What else could she have expected—a full-scale wooing with flowers and dinners for two?

Lisle did all the things she had defiantly promised herself that she would, but it made no difference. No amount of activity could stop her from thinking.

At the end of the week, she decided to swallow her

pride and telephone him. After all, he had told her not to make him wait too long for an answer, even if she still wasn't sure what that answer ought to be.

As she dialled Allard International and waited for the number to ring out, she found she was rehearsing things to say—'Are you sure you want to go through with this marriage?' buzzed in her head, and, 'Please—can't we at least be friends?'

Oh dear, she thought despairingly, I sound so pathetic. Why don't I crawl round there on my knees and beg him to take me?

It was an anti-climax to be told that Jake wasn't there. She replaced the receiver and sat for a moment, thinking. She had got the definite impression, from Gerard, that Jake wasn't expected at Harlow Bannerman for the next few days, but perhaps he was mistaken.

At least Harlow Bannerman was familiar territory, she thought. There was nothing to prevent her going there in person and confronting him. Or at least going there on the ploy of seeing Gerard, or visiting her former colleagues in public relations.

She dressed with care in a high-necked russet wool dress, topping it with her favourite suede coat. As she adjusted the collar, she remembered that she had worn it, for courage, that first night when Jake had come to fetch her.

She looked cool, she thought dispassionately, and sufficiently glamorous. Cosmetics had helped to disguise the effects of daylight fretting and sleepless nights.

As a last touch, she took her engagement ring from the dressing table drawer and replaced it on her finger.

It took all her confidence to get her into the building. The receptionists welcomed her effusively, and promised to phone ahead to Gerard's office to tell him she was on her way up.

But the first person she saw as she stepped out of the

lift was Oliver Grayson. He was looking preoccupied, wearing a slight frown, but when he saw Lisle his face cleared.

'What a wonderful surprise! Is this a social call—or is there something we can do?'

She returned his smile rather more guardedly. 'I came to see Gerard—only I've just realised I don't know where his office is any more now that he's no longer in Sales.'

Oliver's smile faded. 'It's easy to lose track of people nowadays,' he commented acidly.

'So I hear.' Lisle drew a deep breath. 'I understand that you're leaving, Oliver. I'm truly sorry.'

He shrugged. 'These things happen, my dear. I've enjoyed my years at Harlow Bannerman, but the situation I was familiar with has now gone. And I'm not short of offers. A change may not be such a bad thing.'

'You're very philosophical,' she said gently.

'There's no point in being anything else,' he returned. 'It's my choice, after all. As a matter of fact, one of the best offers I've had came from Allard International U.S. I met one of their executives—a man called Sorensen—when he was over recently, and we got on well together.'

'I thought it was the Allard International connection you wanted to sever.' Lisle could not hide her surprise.

Oliver gave her a twisted smile. 'Not altogether. I admire the man if not his methods, and I envy him too—in a number of ways. We had the makings of a good business relationship at first. Perhaps if I'm on the other side of the Atlantic, it can be revived to some extent.'

'I hope so.' Lisle held out her hand. 'Good luck, Oliver.'

He gave her a brooding look. 'Shall I wish you the same, my dear?'

'Perhaps happiness might be more appropriate.' She

made herself smile. 'I'm—I'm lucky already.'

Gerard's new office was a small compartment tucked away in a corner of the managing director's suite. The desk was littered with papers, and a drawer of the filing cabinet stood open, but there was no sign of the occupant.

Lisle peeped in, then made her way back to the main office, where two secretaries were audio typing as if their lives depended on it.

Lisle kept her voice casual. 'My brother's out of his office. Perhaps I could have a word with Mr Allard while I'm waiting.'

'I'm afraid you've missed him, Miss Bannerman. He was here earlier, but he's gone for the day now. But I'm sure Mr Gerard isn't far away, if you'd like to wait in his room.'

Lisle could hardly believe it. For the past hour she had been psyching herself up for this encounter, and now it wasn't going to take place. She wanted very badly to stamp both feet and swear, but she did neither of course.

She said calmly, 'Of course I'll wait,' as if it couldn't matter less, and went back into Gerard's room. It really was very small, she thought, as she settled herself on the only spare chair. Barely room for his desk, and filing cabinet, and the inevitable overflowing waste paper basket.

She glanced at her watch. She'd given him five minutes, then make some excuse and vanish, thus saving a lot of embarrassing explanations, she decided.

In the meantime, there was a newspaper pushed carelessly into the top of the basket, and she leaned forward and retrieved it, opening it casually.

It was folded at the racing pages, and she looked down Gerard's selection for the previous day, wondering wryly whether any of them had won.

She began to turn the pages in a desultory manner, thinking how odd it was that the world kept revolving on its axis just the same, in spite of her unhappiness.

She almost missed the photograph, tucked away at the bottom of a page. It was the headline on the accompanying story which seized her attention. 'No more films for me, says sad Cindy.'

Cindy Leighton didn't look particularly sad. Her smile was aimed straight at the cameras which had met her at Heathrow, where she had landed from the States the day before, her film debut cancelled over problems with the financial backing.

Lisle stared down at the beautiful face, the wide eyes and provocatively parted lips.

'I've come back,' she'd told reporters, 'to pick up the threads of my life where I left off. To hell with Hollywood. Who needs it?'

Lisle drew a deep breath. 'I rather think I did,' she muttered shakily.

Fate, she thought, must be laughing up its sleeve at her. For Cindy to return at this particular time—if she was honest, at any time—was one of life's dirtiest tricks.

And she'd come back *'to pick up the threads'*.

And no doubt the main warp of that design would be Jake.

She looked down at the ring on her hand, trying to derive some comfort from that, but it glittered stonily back at her. It was a token, that was all, and a false token at that, because the bond it was meant to symbolise didn't even exist.

But it will, Lisle told herself. She got to her feet, tossing the newspaper back into the basket, her lips set, and her green eyes flashing fire back at the diamond on her finger.

I'll find him, she thought, and I'll tell him I'll marry him, and somehow I'll make him love me. I'll fill his life so full with passion and tenderness and laughter that there'll be no room for her.

She was through the outer office so fast, the girls hardly noticed her passing. In the street, she hailed a cruising cab with a feeling of thankfulness.

'Who says there are never taxis when you need them?' she thought as she gave the driver the address of Jake's flat.

He had either just arrived, or was just leaving, because his car was parked across the entrance.

Lisle's driver drew in at the other side of the road, and slid back the glass partition so that she could pay him.

As it turned out, Jake was leaving. He came out of the building, carrying a suitcase, and walked towards the car. Cindy Leighton was with him, walking at his side, her arm hugging his with open possession, her mane of blonde hair gleaming in the thin winter sunlight.

She looked as if she had the world at her feet. Lisle's world.

She sat unmoving in the taxi, and watched them drive away together.

CHAPTER TEN

'ARE you sure you're all right?' Janie asked for perhaps the seventh time.

'Yes, of course.' Lisle smiled steadily. 'I just need to get away for a few days, that's all. It's very good of Graham to lend me the cottage.'

Janie shrugged. 'Well, he and Sally rarely use it after October. He told me that you were to finish up anything left in the freezer. He thinks there's some fish and a couple of chickens. You can buy your vegetables locally.'

Lisle looked down at the things she was packing. 'I don't suppose I shall be doing much cooking.'

Janie gave her an alarmed look. 'But you must eat! You'll make yourself ill, otherwise, and the cottage is pretty isolated.' She bit her lip. 'In fact the more I think about it, the less it seems a good idea. Why don't you get some winter sunshine instead? Grab a package tour of some kind—go somewhere cheerful—meet people. What good is it going to do to vanish into the depths of the country and brood?'

Lisle folded a blouse fiercely. 'None whatever, probably. But it's what I want, Janie. It's what I need. I want to be somewhere no one can find me.'

'And who is included under the heading of no one?' Janie asked.

Lisle's mouth tightened. 'Everyone, I suppose. Please don't tell Gerard for a start.'

'I've no intention of doing so,' Janie said calmly. 'He'd derive far too much satisfaction from the situation. As far as he's concerned, you've gone away by yourself for a few days to think things out.' She paused. 'And if Jake Allard starts making enquiries—what then?'

174

'It's hardly likely.' Lisle's voice shook a little. 'He's—occupied in other directions, remember?'

'As if I could forget,' Janie muttered. 'I'll never get over the way you looked when you came into the office. For a moment I hardly recognised you.'

'I've hardly recognised myself for quite a while,' Lisle said drily. 'It was good of Graham to give you the rest of the afternoon off.'

'He was as worried as I was. He doesn't know about the Leighton woman, of course. I told him you were still suffering the emotional after-effects of losing your grandfather.' She hesitated. 'Lisle, why don't you stay here—at the Priory?'

Lisle shook her head. 'Because I can't lose myself here. As soon as Gerard reads the note I left him, he'll be telephoning here, probably wanting to come down. I don't want anyone to find me—especially the Press, if the story of Jake's reunion with Cindy Leighton gets out.'

'I hadn't thought of that,' Janie conceded. She sighed. 'But I'm still not sure whether running away is the right thing to do. Why not stay and fight?'

'Because I don't think I'd win.' Lisle fastened the case. 'I seem to have done nothing but pack and unpack for weeks. It will be nice just to—settle for a little while.'

'Well, you keep listening to the wireless, and if they forecast snow, get out fast,' Janie advised dourly.

Lisle hugged her impulsively. 'Janie, you've been an angel. I don't know what I'd have done without you. I—I hate unloading my troubles on to you like this. . . .'

'Rubbish,' Janie said roundly, returning the hug. 'You can return the favour some day.'

'I hope it won't be necessary,' Lisle gave her a long look.

Janie shrugged. 'I hope not too, but I'm counting on nothing,' she countered with a little crooked smile.

'Gerard is still using my shoulder to cry on at the moment. Perhaps there'll come a time when he discovers I have other uses. That, or another Carla Foxton will come along,' she added candidly.

Two hours later, Lisle had reached the cottage. It was more than a mile from the nearest village, reached by a very narrow lane, and she eased the Mini along carefully, hoping she wouldn't meet another vehicle round the next bend.

It was a pretty place, she decided, as she parked the car. Built of old mellow brick, its low slate roof, encrusted here and there with lichen, swooped down over narrow casement windows set under gables. There was a small, overgrown garden at the front, and an orchard at the rear leading down to a stream.

As Lisle walked up the path to the front door, she could hear the beguiling sound of running water. But not much else. If she had come to find peace and quiet, certainly it was waiting for her there.

The cottage itself smelt musty, having been closed up for several weeks, but there was no telltale smell of damp. Graham, and his wife, spent most of their weekends there, Lisle knew, and had spent a considerable amount on restoration and modernisation.

The kitchen and tiny bathroom paid tribute to their efforts, she thought, as she looked around, and the furnishing and decoration contributed strongly to the character of the place.

There were three bedrooms upstairs, and Lisle chose the smallest, normally used by Joanna, Graham's teenage daughter. The walls were checkered with posters of pop stars, and there were books, many of which Lisle herself had owned when she was younger, crammed on to the deep windowsill.

Lisle had stopped in the village and bought some milk, eggs and bread, and she put these away in the kitchen, before unbolting the back door and taking a look at the rest of her small domain.

There was a good store of wood under cover at the rear, and she filled a basket with logs and kindling and carried it back into the house to light the woodstove which warmed the living room. It was soon crackling cheerfully, and she made toast and scrambled a couple of eggs she had bought, eating the simple meal beside the stove, with the first book of Tolkien's *Lord of the Rings* propped up beside her as she ate. It was a favourite of hers, and she had read it several times before, but the adventures and perils of the hobbits and their companions failed to exercise their usual magic.

All she could see in her mind's eye was Cindy Leighton's blonde head close to Jake's dark one, and her triumphant smile.

I haven't really run away at all, she thought, because I've brought them with me.

There was no television at the cottage, but she switched on the radio and listened to a play, and then some music. And when she mounted the stairs to her small room with its sloping ceiling, there was the distant rush of the stream to soothe her, if not to sleep, then at least to a semblance of tranquillity.

The weather was mild and damp, and she took the opportunity of working in the garden, weeding, tidying and tying back. It was one way, she thought, of thanking Sally and Graham for allowing her to stay there, because Graham had refused point blank to accept any kind of rent from her.

No one came. Once two magpies perched on the fence and watched her.

'One of you shouldn't be there,' she told them as she went indoors to make herself some coffee.

The postman came, bringing the usual clutch of circulars for the occupier, and a letter from Janie for Lisle. It was brief, cheerful and chatty, but it was the laconic postscript which made Lisle think. It said simply, 'Enquiries about you are being pursued. My lips are sealed.'

Lisle sighed. Bless you, Janie, she thought.

By the fourth day, the damp weather had deteriorated into a steady downpour which showed no signs of easing. Lisle banked up the stove and went into the village for supplies. She dawdled over her shopping, buying spices and cream to make the thawing chicken back at the cottage more interesting, and treating herself to a bottle of wine from the post office, which doubled as an off-licence.

She had just turned into the lane on her way back when she realised a car was following her.

Her first thought was that it was a mistake. The lane led nowhere except to the cottage.

Her second, shattering realisation was that it was Jake's car.

Lisle swallowed, her hands tightening on the wheel, then she put her foot down and her own vehicle leapt forward.

And if we meet a tractor, she thought hysterically, then it's just too bad.

But the lane was deserted as usual. She braked recklessly outside the cottage, and almost flung herself out of the car, leaving her shopping where it was, her one intent to get into the house and lock herself in.

But the path was slippery with rain, and she slipped and fell down on to one knee, costing herself any headway she had made against him.

Jake took her by the shoulders and lifted her to her feet.

'Little fool!' His voice was bleak with rage. 'I'll take that.'

With one swift movement, he had dispossessed her of the key. Holding her firmly by the arm, he marched her to the front door.

Lisle struggled unavailingly. 'Let go of me!'

'Make me,' he suggested. He opened the door and

thrust her roughly inside. 'Or better still, get your lover to do it. Where is he, by the way? Still sleeping off the pleasures of last night?'

'What the hell are you talking about?' Lisle whirled round, facing him furiously, her rounded breasts rising and falling stormily under the force of her emotions.

'I'm talking about Grayson, of course. I'm going to break his bloody neck!'

She stared at him, really seeing him, seeing the grey tinge to his skin, the deep shadows under his eyes, the tense, strained lines round his mouth. She thought, 'He looks almost worse than I do.'

She said slowly, 'Oliver? You were expecting to see Oliver? But that's ridiculous!'

'Is it?' His voice sneered, the dark face full of bitter challenge and he looked at her. 'Why else would you engage in this conspiracy of silence—sneak off to this romantic little love nest, if not to be with him—or someone else? Don't play the innocent, Lisle,' he added roughly. 'I'll find him, if I have to tear the place apart, and when I do. . . .'

'But you won't,' she said. 'Because he isn't here. I'm quite alone. That's how I wanted it, and that's how it is.'

He laughed. 'I said before you were a good actress, beauty. But you can drop the role-playing now. You've condemned yourself out of your own mouth.' He took a folded paper out of his pocket. 'Remember this?'

She frowned. 'It looks like the note I left for Gerard. But how . . .?'

'How did I get hold of it? He gave it to me. Oh, he didn't want to,' he added, his mouth twisting. 'He was most reluctant. Even inclined to blame himself to some extent for your—proclivities.'

Lisle said, 'I don't understand one word of this. I don't see why Gerard should have shown you my note, but on the other hand there was nothing in it that you shouldn't see.'

His brows lifted. 'No? Perhaps you'd better refresh your memory.'

He handed it to her, and she unfolded the paper, her eyes flicking wonderingly over the few brief lines. She knew them by heart, of course.

'Dear Gerard,' she'd written, 'Please don't worry about me. I need to get out of London for a while and so I'm going away.

'Don't try to look for me. Lisle.'

It was on the second reading that she realised incredulously that someone had added the damning words 'with Oliver' at the end of the first paragraph. Someone. . . .

She went very white. She said. 'This isn't what I wrote. It's been doctored.'

'Of course,' he sneered. 'And the fact that Grayson was leaving your flat the night of my mother's dinner party, and you were saying goodbye to him half-dressed, is just sheer coincidence. And so, I suppose, is the way you just happened to meet at Harlow Bannerman a few days ago, and the curious circum-stance that he hasn't been at the office since. He rang in claiming to have a virus.' He added, his mouth curling, 'What kind of a fool do you think I am?'

She said desperately, 'I've never thought that, Jake. Oliver was at the flat that night—yes—because he found Gerard and brought him there. No other reason. And I did talk to him the other day, but only for a few minutes. I've no idea where he's been since, or what he's doing. You have to believe me.'

'I've tried to believe you.' His voice sounded grim and defeated. 'Over and over again, I've kept hoping. I even told myself that the withdrawal I sensed when you were in my arms was shyness—even innocence. But you soon disillusioned me about that, beauty.'

She looked at him, stunned, remembering, but at the same time conscious of the first stirrings of anger deep inside.

She said, 'Search the place if you want. I won't stop you, I couldn't anyway. But how dare you accuse me? Who gives you the right to operate a double standard?'

'What the hell are you talking about?'

'Your—friend,' she burst out. 'Miss Leighton. It didn't take long for you to get together again. I suppose you met her while you were in America too.'

'No.' The grey eyes narrowed searchingly. 'So it was you. I noticed the taxi across the road as I came out, and wondered why it took off like a rocket a minute later. Was this cosy few days with Grayson your notion of revenge?'

'I don't need revenge,' she said stonily. 'It's immaterial to me what you do. I—I came to the flat that day to tell you I'd decided not to marry you. So we're both free now—to live in any way that we want. Perhaps in the circumstances you'll leave.'

'I'll leave when I'm good and ready,' said Jake on a snarl. 'You're determined to make a mess of your life, aren't you, Lisle?'

'By not marrying you?' She gave an uneven laugh. 'What a king-sized ego you have! Miss Leighton's devotion must have gone to your head.'

'We'll leave Cindy out of this, if you don't mind.' The level voice held a steely note. 'We're discussing your relationship with Oliver Grayson.'

'I have no relationship with him!' Her voice rose angrily. 'And he's not here. Look round if you don't believe me.'

There was a long heavy pause, then he went past her and up the stairs.

Lisle's legs were shaking. She backed to a chair and sat down.

She heard him moving around, then his footsteps on the uncarpeted staircase.

She didn't look up.

He said quietly, 'I accept that you're alone here, Lisle. Why, then, did you tell your brother you were coming away with Grayson? For Pete's sake, why?'

She said wearily, 'I didn't. Gerard must have added that bit himself. Apparently he's been blaming you for losing him Carla Foxton. Showing you my note with embellishments must have been his idea of getting his own back.' She added stonily, 'He thought, you see, that we were still going to be married.'

'And so we are,' he said harshly. 'I won't take no for an answer, Lisle.'

'You'll have to.' Her eyes were fierce and bright as they met his. 'Because I was so lacking in pride when I agreed to this charade initially it doesn't mean I'm prepared to tie myself legally to some other woman's man.' She threw her head back. 'I don't need your charity, Jake. I'll make out somehow. You keep pushing my relationship with Oliver—perhaps I'll ask him to take me to the States as his assistant.'

He said softly, 'You go anywhere near him, and there'll be no job in the States. I'll see to that.'

'Oh, you're a bastard!' Her voice shook. 'Now will you get out of here, and leave me in peace.'

'Peace!' Jake repeated, and gave a short laugh. 'There's been no peace for either of us ever since we met. I can't think straight, I can't work, I can't sleep, and it's all down to you, beauty.' The grey eyes went over her. 'Even if you won't marry me, I think you owe me some kind of recompense for the hell of the past few weeks.' He reached for her, pulling her to her feet.

She said huskily, 'Take your hands off me.'

'That tremulous note is wonderfully authentic,' he said. 'But this time it isn't going to work. I want you, and I'm going to have you, so keep the virginal reluctance for some other fool. We both know that it doesn't mean a damned thing.'

He kissed her savagely, forcing her lips apart with his.

For a moment she struggled, her hands beating in a

frenzy against his shoulders, and the unyielding wall of his chest, then, with a little moan, she capitulated, responding helplessly to the harsh demand of his mouth.

At once his kiss gentled. His lips moved on hers with an aching, passionate tenderness which made her tremble as her arms went slowly round his neck to hold him close.

He cupped her face in his hands, the grey eyes very brilliant.

He said softly, 'The battle's over, Lisle. We belong together, and I won't let you go.'

He was shaking too, and although his hands were gentle, his touch seemed to scorch her to the bone.

He unfastened her coat and slid it from her shoulders, tossing it on to a nearby chair. Then he walked to the cottage door and locked it with a kind of cool deliberation.

Lisle stood very still. The rushing of the nearby stream sounded almost thunderous in the enclosed quiet of the room. Or perhaps it was only the sound of her own blood she could hear as Jake came back, swiftly and silently, to her side.

He picked her up in his arms and carried her over to the sofa, holding her close while he kissed her softly and sensuously, his mouth brushing her temples and cheekbones, the line of her jaw and the tender lobes of her ears.

She clung to him with a kind of desperation, trying to ignore the little voice inside her which was reminding her where all this was inevitably leading.

Jake said gently, 'Relax, darling. We're making love, not war, remember?'

She looked up at him, trying to smile, wondering if the sick panic within her was showing in her eyes.

She said insanely, 'We—we can't. . . . It's broad daylight!'

His own expression was wry. 'So it is. Does that

make a difference? Or is it another ploy to keep me at arm's length.'

'No—at least—I don't know.' She drew a deep, quivering breath. 'Oh, you wouldn't understand.'

'Try me,' he invited quietly.

She moved away from him, out of his arms, putting space between them. She didn't look at him.

She said, 'I know what you think about me, Jake—about the way I've led my life. I know what you've always thought. But it isn't true—not any of it.' She tried to smile. 'It could have been, I suppose, but that wasn't what I wanted. Or perhaps I just wasn't capable. ... Gerard used to laugh at me,' she added painfully. Jake said something under his breath and Lisle winced, turning her head away. 'Oh, I knew you wouldn't believe me.'

The long fingers captured her chin, making her face him. 'Why do you say that? As it happens, I do believe you. It makes sudden sense out of the muddle which has always existed between us. But why didn't you tell me before, Lisle? And why are you telling me now?'

'Does it matter?' She spoke unevenly.

'If it didn't, I wouldn't be asking,' he said rather grimly.

The intensity of his gaze was overwhelming, and she closed her eyes, swallowing weakly.

She said, 'Because at first, it didn't matter. I didn't care what you thought of me. ...'

'And now?' His hand caressed her soft throat, seeking the tumult of her pulse. 'Look at me, sweetheart.'

She obeyed on a little indrawn breath as she saw the look in his eyes.

Jake said softly, 'I love you, Lisle. And I'm beginning to hope—to believe that you love me. Could that be why all this matters so desperately to both of us?'

She said with a kind of desperation, 'You don't love me—you can't—when there's Cindy Leighton, and those others. ...'

'Dear heavens!' Jake groaned. 'You make it sound as if my life has been an unending rake's progress. Perhaps it's time this burst of honesty became mutual. Yes, Cindy and I were lovers—but only for a short time, and it was over before you and I ever met. However, we parted amicably and have remained friends.'

'Friends?' Lisle pushed away his caressing hand. 'How can you say that? I saw you together, and she was living with you at your flat before she went to America.'

'Yes, she stayed at the flat, but not with me. There was a short lapse of time between the giving up of the lease on her own place and her actual departure, and she asked if she could stay at the flat.' He gave Lisle a level look. 'Perhaps she was planning a romantic interlude as a farewell, but I wasn't interested in finding out. I moved out, and went to stay at a hotel.' He stroked her cheek with his finger. 'If you want to verify it, you can.'

'But she came back from America,' Lisle protested feebly. 'She told the newspapers she was going to "pick up the threads". I thought. . . .'

'I can guess what you thought,' he said. 'But Cindy's overriding interest at the moment is her abortive career in films. She contacted me because she wanted a shoulder to cry on, admittedly, but I told her I had troubles of my own. However, I think she could make a success in films, given the right opportunity, and I promised her I'd introduce her to a friend of mine who could help. That's where I was taking her when you saw us—to join his house party in Surrey, and discuss the possibility of a new contract. As far as I know, she's still there.' He smiled at her. 'Now, do you believe me? Do you believe that since the moment I first saw you, I've wanted no one else?'

Her lips parted helplessly. 'But you thought all those things about me. You despised me.'

'I wanted to. When Murray first broached the idea of a marriage between us, I was all set to reject it out of hand. I didn't even want to meet you. Then his illness forced us together, and I was lost no matter how hard I tried to fight it. And I did try.'

'Yes,' her voice shook. 'I've been so unhappy. . . .'

Jake drew her back into his arms. 'It's probably no consolation, darling, but I've been wretched too. Particularly when you kept flaunting Oliver Grayson at me. I was terrified that you were going to elope with the poor devil.' He grimaced. 'I thought that was what—this,' he gestured at the sheltering walls around them, 'was all about. Driving down here was the worst journey of my life.'

Lisle said, 'Poor Oliver. Neither of us has been very fair to him.'

'We haven't been fair to each other.' He lifted her hand to his lips, kissing each finger in turn. 'You aren't wearing your ring.'

She said shyly, 'It's upstairs. I felt it was wrong to wear it when everything was so—uncertain.'

'But you're not uncertain any more?' He gave her a long, searching look. 'And you'll marry me as soon as I can get a licence?'

'Oh, yes!' She smiled up at him, all concealment fled, love for him luminous in her green eyes. 'And don't you think this would make a wonderful place for a honeymoon?'

'It might at that.' He glanced round, smiling faintly. 'Do you want me to see if it can be arranged?'

She said on a little catch of her breath, 'But there's nothing to arrange. You're here and so am I. What else do we need for a honeymoon?'

Jake was very still for a moment, then he said slowly, 'Nothing at all.' He cupped her face in his hands, the grey eyes warm and steady as he looked down at her. 'You're sure you wouldn't prefer to be virtuously driven back to London to wait for the wedding—the ceremony, the ring, the champagne, the whole bit?'

'Quite sure.' She put her arms round his neck, drawing him down to her, her body melting as she sensed his mounting hunger. 'I love you, Jake. Isn't that all that matters?'

'It's the whole world,' he told her huskily. 'My dear love. . . .'

TREACLE TART

When Lisle goes home to the Priory she is greeted warmly by Mrs. Peterson. One of the first things "Petey" does for Lisle is serve her a delicious meal whose finishing touch is "a slice of homemade treacle tart, accompanied by thickly whipped cream."

Treacle is a popular British food that closely resembles molasses and is sometimes referred to as "golden syrup"; "tart," of course, is what the British call "pie." Treacle tart, then, is essentially an open-faced pie with a treacle and breadcrumb filling.

To make your own treacle tart, beat an egg with a teaspoon of water and combine it with 2 cups of treacle (you may substitute molasses), 1½ cups fresh white breadcrumbs and a teaspoon of lemon juice. Spread the mixture over a 9-inch pastry shell, and use additional pastry to make a lattice-work topping. Bake at 325°F. (165°C.) for approximately 30 minutes. Serve hot with whipped cream.

Rich, loaded with calories—but absolutely delicious!

HARLEQUIN
PREMIERE AUTHOR EDITIONS

6 top Harlequin authors — 6 of their best books!

1. JANET DAILEY Giant of Mesabi
2. CHARLOTTE LAMB Dark Master
3. ROBERTA LEIGH Heart of the Lion
4. ANNE MATHER Legacy of the Past
5. ANNE WEALE Stowaway
6. VIOLET WINSPEAR The Burning Sands

**Harlequin is proud to offer these 6 exciting romance novels by
6 of our most popular authors. In brand-new beautifully
designed covers, each Harlequin Premiere Author Edition
is a bestselling love story—a contemporary, compelling and
passionate read to remember!**

Available wherever paperback books are sold, *or* through
Harlequin Reader Service. Simply complete and mail the coupon below.

- -

1